A
Country Doctor
AND THE
Epidemics
⋙ *Montana 1917–1918* ⋘

⋙ A Historical Novella ⋘
BY STEVEN D. HELGERSON

Front cover photo: Forsyth, MT. Main Street at corner of 9th. Courtesy Montana Historical Society Research Center. PAC 76-26 F13.

Back cover photo: Rosebud County, country road. Courtesy Montana Historical Society Research Center. PAC 76-26-192

ISBN 13: 978-1-59152-191-4

Published by Steven D. Helgerson

You may order extra copies of this book by calling Farcountry Press toll free at (800) 821-3874.

sweetgrassbooks
an imprint of Farcountry Press

Produced by Sweetgrass Books.
PO Box 5630, Helena, MT 59604; (800) 821-3874; www.sweetgrassbooks.com.

The views expressed by the author/publisher in this book do not necessarily represent the views of, nor should be attributed to, Sweetgrass Books. Sweetgrass Books is not responsible for the content of the author/publisher's work.

 Produced and printed in the United States of America.

21   20   19   18   17   1   2   3   4   5

"From time immemorial human life has been cursed by the two great evils of war and pestilence. Working at times together, at times apart, there is no portion of the earth and no race of men that they have not devastated."
—LEE, F. S. *SCIENTIFIC FEATURES OF MODERN MEDICINE.*
COLUMBIA UNIVERSITY PRESS, NEW YORK. 1911.

"Xenophobia is a disease more dangerous to a free people than a physical plague. If a political Pasteur could tell the world how to isolate and destroy the indiscriminate hatred of other nationals or other races...he would bring to mankind a blessing of which it is greatly in need at the present hour."
—"XENOPHOBIA" (EDITORIAL), *NEW YORK TIMES,*
JANUARY 9, 1923, PAGE 22.

Table of Contents

Foreword

The story told in this novella is fiction, although many of the events are consistent with actual events in 1917 and 1918. The setting is based on Rosebud County and Forsyth, Montana, as they existed during those years.

Readers will learn of a fictional physician who provided contemporary medical care but was troubled by the stark limitations of medical science to treat many of the diseases he encountered, including epidemic disease.

The dialogue is fiction but reflective of the events of the time. Some characters—such as a state legislator, a sheriff, a county commissioner, and a county school superintendent—existed, but the names and all statements made by these characters in this story come entirely from the imagination of the author. Other characters are composites; these include a rancher, a homesteader, a banker, a waitress, and a public health nurse. Statements made by these characters also come from the author's imagination. Patients seen by the physician are fictional, although the medical conditions and the treatments described reflect medical practice in 1917 and 1918.

The behaviors stimulated by fear, anxiety, and beliefs related to war and disease described in this story were not unique to the early twentieth century.

CHAPTER ONE

December 31, 1918

Why can't I open my eyes? Doctor Harvey thought. He sat uncomfortably in a straight-backed chair with his hands folded in his lap. There were two women in the room, and they were talking about him. They spoke as if he was not there.

"Very unusual case," one woman said. "Only one like this I've seen during my years as a nurse at Deaconess Hospital."

The other woman said, "I heard the doctors talking at rounds this morning. They said this case is a mystery."

"The patient is a doctor, you know," the first woman said. "He was transported to Billings from Forsyth because there is no hospital there."

"Now there is one less doctor there, too," said the second woman. "I wonder what's happened to him?"

Doctor Harvey, eyes closed, sat motionless, recalling Forsyth and his work there.

CHAPTER TWO

April 21, 1917

A neatly dressed woman stood on the railway station landing waving a banner that said, "Halt the Hun."

The crowd cheered as the Northern Pacific No. 3 engine began its slow roll from the station, heading west to Billings. Children clung shyly to their mothers' dresses, most of which were made of cotton but some store-bought gingham and gabardine. Mothers and fathers, sisters and brothers, friends and neighbors waved at the seven young men onboard.

It seemed everyone in town had gathered at the Forsyth Club in the Masonic building that Saturday evening to show their support for the boys. They'd enlisted in the National Guard and were on their way to Fort Harrison to prepare for active duty and deployment. Speeches by State Senator Edwards and District Judge Crum as well as rousing marches by the Forsyth Concert Band had highlighted the send-off. The soldiers-to-be appeared eager to embark on their journey "over there."

Doctor Harvey watched the gathering from the sidewalk on Main Street opposite the railway station. During the weeks since the *Forsyth Times-Journal* had announced "War Resolution Passes," he had listened to patriotic declarations by townspeople in stores, the saloon, the bank, his office, and at church. It seemed even God intended for the United States to enter and end this war. The conflict had been enormously lethal—though mostly stationary for three years already since an archduke was assassinated in Sarajevo in 1914. Few in this riverside

Montana town had known where Sarajevo was, let alone what griev-ances might have led an angry young Bosnian Serb man to assassinate an archduke and his wife. Now, however, young Montana men were joining thousands more from across the United States to be uniformed, trained, and transported to trenches to join Allied troops and fight oth-er young men from countries called "the Central Powers."

The train pulled away from the station and crossed the road on the western edge of Forsyth. The conductor sounded the whistle, warning automobiles and horse-drawn wagons to stay off the railway tracks. It seemed appropriate to Doctor Harvey for a train transporting men to war to blast an announcement so consistent with the nation's policy: out of our way while we make the world safe for democracy. He won-dered how many of the eager young men would return to Forsyth and Rosebud County.

Not everyone had endorsed a declaration of war. Montana's Representative Jeannette Rankin, the first and only woman elected to the U.S. Congress, had voted against entering the war. She was vilified by many for her vote. Yet she, along with almost all Americans, sup-ported the mobilization needed for war. Still, concern about sedition and espionage was fueling discussion in Congress—and among some on that railway landing in Forsyth. A week earlier, the *Forsyth Times-Journal* published a proclamation from County Sheriff Harold Starr guaranteeing safety to foreign-born residents as long as they were law-abiding. It also promised prompt action against those who rendered aid or comfort to the enemy.

The crowd began to disperse, and a rancher and his wife and daughters strode to their automobile. They were headed home to their thousand-acre ranch west of town where they had raised sheep in the 1890s; after some drought years and decreased sheep production, they switched to grazing cattle and horses and growing hay and grain crops. The rancher irrigated the crops with water from a ditch he and neighbors had dug to take water from the Yellowstone River. Like other ranchers in eastern Montana, he had increased wheat acreage in response to rapidly grow-ing demand to support war mobilization. Doctor Harvey imagined that before traveling to the railway station, this family had likely spent that spring afternoon tending to some cattle, a couple of milk cows, and the beginnings of a garden from which they would harvest delicious beans, peas, carrots, and tomatoes during the summer and squash in the autumn.

Most folks walked north from the railway landing across Main Street toward the buildings where most of the town's commerce and entertainment took place. These buildings were dispersed as if on a string east to west on the north side of Main Street parallel to the railroad tracks. The laying of the Northern Pacific Railroad tracks near the south bank of the Yellowstone River in 1883 had led to the establishment and growth of many string towns. These towns benefitted from the reliable transportation while allowing the railway company to prosper. With a population of 2,100, Forsyth was the largest of the railroad towns between Miles City and Billings.

As Doctor Harvey watched the crowd disperse, he thought, *even the old-timers here are newcomers.* Indigenous people had traveled and camped in what became Montana for hundreds of years. Two tribes of these people, the Crow and the Northern Cheyenne, now lived geographically restricted lives on reservations southwest and south of town. A century and a decade ago, William Clark and a portion of the Lewis and Clark Corps of Discovery camped near the present-day site of Forsyth on their return trip to tell President Jefferson of their journey to the Pacific Ocean. The magnificent mountains they had crossed on that journey were far to the west; from here no mountains were visible, even from the high plains plateaus that rose 100 to 200 feet on either side of the Yellowstone River. But even the oldest of the large cattle and sheep ranches in this area was only a few decades old, and Forsyth— established as a steamboat landing in 1876 and designated with a post office in 1882—did not become a county seat until 1901.

Doctor Harvey recalled that it had not taken long to become acquainted with downtown; there were only a few blocks of it. He was standing near Ninth Avenue in front of the Alexander Hotel, in which he had leased a room since relocating to Forsyth earlier that year. Like most buildings on Main Street from Eighth to Eleventh Avenues—the core of downtown—this hotel was a two-story building. Around the corner on one side of Ninth was a wholesale liquor business, and on the other side a mercantile store that sold clothing as well as hardware and furniture. Also on Ninth near Main was a café. One block west, at the corner of Eighth Avenue and Main Street, was the three-story Commercial Hotel, which advertised itself as "A thoroughly modern brick hotel" with electric lights, steam heat, telephones, and baths as well as the "only sample rooms in town."

Although the Alexander Hotel might not have been as thoroughly modern as the Commercial Hotel, it was entirely adequate for Doctor Harvey, with its electricity, telephones, and indoor running water. Traveling railroad personnel often stayed here. East of the Alexander Hotel was a pharmacy, a menswear store, a bank, and a meat market. Farther east, at the corner of Tenth and Main, was a garage and automobile sales business; still farther east the Masonic Temple with its square and compass emblem prominently displayed on the second-floor façade. At the edge of town, just two blocks east of Tenth Avenue near Main Street, was the neoclassical courthouse topped by a copper dome and completed in 1914.

Among the first to cross Main Street from the railway station was a neatly trimmed, medium-build, middle-aged man who worked as a cashier at one of the two banks in town. He called out, "Good evening, Doctor."

"Good evening," he replied.

"We gave our boys a good send-off today. They'll have the Hun on the run in short order," the banker said confidently.

"I hope the war is over soon," Doctor Harvey replied, less assured.

"Well, we'll have more boys ready to go if they are needed. We'll fill our quota when the draft kicks in."

Doctor Harvey replied, "If I understand correctly, young men twenty-one to thirty years in age may be drafted. Do you anticipate volunteers older or younger than that?"

"I think the boys who left today, except maybe the Matte boy, were in the draft age group. Some might be thinking they'll have better choices as volunteers now than they would as draftees later." The banker continued, "Now Matte, he's just eighteen but plumb convinced he's the best shot in Rosebud County. He'll need to be reminded to keep his head down."

In turn Doctor Harvey observed, "Some prominent physicians

around the country, including Doctor Huene, from here as you know, have volunteered for the Army Medical Corps. Still, I suspect young, draft-age doctors will be needed soon enough."

"Well, I'm glad you are more than thirty, and I hope you don't go volunteering, too. We need doctors at home as well as at the front in Europe," said the banker, who had guessed correctly about Doctor Harvey's age.

"I'm not thinking to volunteer," he said.

"I'm more concerned about the Germans living here than I am about filling our quota of boys to go over there," emphasized the banker. "I don't think it is safe to have Krauts walking around our town."

Doctor Harvey did not reply but thought of a German rancher, Herman Mueller, to whom he had provided medical care. Mr. Mueller ranched west of town on several hundred acres of very fertile river valley land along the Yellowstone River. His parents had established a foothold on 160 acres of this land in the 1880s and subsequently managed to purchase additional acreage. By the time Herman, the oldest of four children and only son in the family, had assumed the lead role in the operation, the ranch had grown to several hundred acres. In 1916, stimulated by growing demand for grain crops, he had borrowed money from one of the local banks in order to purchase wheat seed and fertilizer. Now he had already become concerned about continuing increases in grain seed prices and whether he might need to seek another loan for planting this year.

The banker continued, "It's bad enough to have Rankin vote against going to war. How can our country protect freedom when we send a woman to Congress and she has a female hysterical fit? It's worse yet to have supporters of the Kaiser walking our streets."

Doctor Harvey observed, "A half dozen senators and more than a dozen representatives also voted no; they were all men." He preferred not to respond to the idea that neighbors might undermine the nation's war effort and was relieved to hear another greeting.

"It's so nice to see you this lovely evening," chimed the wife of the pastor at one of Forsyth's churches. "We are all so proud of the young men and so thankful to them for protecting us." She was a plump, middle-aged woman who was loved, or at least appreciated, by all for her tireless effort to support not only members of her Methodist congregation but also those in need throughout the community.

Then another voice boomed when a stately man dressed in a dark-gray suit and a red, white, and blue tie joined the banker, the doctor, and the pastor's wife on the sidewalk. "Today is the day Forsyth joined the fight! I hope other legislators are seeing the same commitment in their communities as I am so proud to see here," said Arthur Elliott, a legislator who had represented the district for more than ten years. "It's time to address issues other than alcohol. Hasn't the Women's Christian Temperance Union done enough already? Isn't beer doubly bad? It's both alcohol and German!"

Elliott, who by his own telling was one of the state's most influential legislators—although characterized by opponents as exercising influence by being one of the least scrupulous as well—began to elaborate, "I'm in a position to gather the votes needed to..."

He was interrupted by a horse-drawn wagon carrying several boisterous men stopped on the street near the legislator. The men were singing the national anthem out of tune and waving the American flag.

The sight of the wagon on Main Street prompted Doctor Harvey to recall another wagon arriving here four days ago. That wagon pulled by two sweat-soaked, rapid-breathing horses had come to a quick stop near the sidewalk where Doctor Harvey had been standing.

A frightened driver shouted, "Doctor, my brother is hurt. Please help."

Doctor Harvey quickly stepped off the sidewalk in order to examine the blanket-wrapped bundle from which protruded only a shock of light-brown hair atop the very pale, unmoving face of a seven-year-old boy. Holding the bundled boy was a thin woman about thirty years of age with a distressed look on her otherwise attractive face. As he unwrapped the blanket, he quickly noticed a portion that covered the boy's legs was caked with dried blood. He glanced back at the woman.

Tears streamed down her face as she pleaded, "Please help my son. He fell. I think his leg is broken. I couldn't get him here any faster. Please help."

Doctor Harvey took the woman's hand and asked her to hold her son a little longer. He then said firmly to two men in the gathering crowd, "Please help me get this boy into my office, then take the horses to the livery for some water."

He looked at the mother and asked, "What is the boy's name? And what is your name?"

The woman wiped away tears from her face and replied, "I am Mrs. Swensen, Amanda Swensen, and this is Raymond." She looked at the young man driving the wagon and said, "This is my son Axel."

CHAPTER THREE

April 17, 1917
Early Afternoon

Doctor Harvey laid the boy on the exam table in his office. The suite consisted of an entry room where patients registered with his assistant, Margaret May (who preferred to be called May); a small room with a microscope, some medications, and reference textbooks; and a larger room for patient examination. May helped remove the blood-stained blanket and glanced at Doctor Harvey, who said, "Please take Mrs. Swensen to the entry area and give her some water and a wet towel to cool her face."

Using scissors he cut the boy's right trouser leg to view the wound more completely. A jagged-edge laceration began a few inches above the ankle and extended upward about five inches on the right side of the leg. Raymond was pale and moaned when Doctor Harvey began to explore and clean the wound. No bone was visible. Despite the swollen tissue, he palpated an area of fracture of the tibia above the ankle.

May returned to the exam room and placed two basins filled with warm water beside the table. Doctor Harvey used the water to clean the skin and irrigate the wound profusely. He knew this open wound was a high risk for infection and further irrigated the wound with a solution of peroxide. For a moment he wished he had access to x-ray equipment but quickly resolved to set the fracture as carefully as he could. He asked May to bring a container of chloroform from the medication cabinet.

He placed his hand on Raymond's shoulder and said, "You are a strong lad. I want you to count backwards from ten while I hold this cloth near your nose. It will help you to rest. When you wake up you may feel some pain where I set your bone." Raymond was already unconscious.

After he aligned the ends of the tibia as closely as he could discern by careful palpation, he approximated the skin wound edges and inserted several stitches. He cleaned the skin around the wound again and placed a bandage. Now he could apply a splint from above the knee to below the ankle, leaving just enough access to the wound site so it could be cleaned and newly bandaged at intervals.

Before beginning the splint placement, he said to May, "Please go and reassure Mrs. Swensen. Her son is resting now but it will be a few more minutes before he can be moved. Ask her if she knows someone in town with whom she could stay for several days so we can monitor the wound healing and keep the area clean while it heals."

May went into the entry area, and Doctor Harvey took a deep breath. He looked at the framed diploma mounted on the wall near the exam table. It read, "Northwestern University School of Medicine awards the degree of Doctor of Medicine to Kelly K. Harvey this thirtieth day of May, 1913." He had not completed medical education until he was twenty-eight years of age. Following college graduation from the University of Illinois in 1906, he had returned to his family's farm. His father had died months before; a wagon loaded with hay had tipped onto him while he had tried to keep it upright on a sharply sloped area of the field. His mother died almost exactly one year later of tuberculosis. With his older brother he had kept the farm in operation and also had worked as an assistant to a local veterinarian. The latter work had sparked his interest in medical practice. After his brother married and brought his wife to live in the family's farmhouse, Kelly, who had never aspired to be a farmer, resolved to pursue medical training.

He thought back to Chicago and Northwestern where he studied for three years before completing an internship in 1914. He recalled anatomy, physiology, and pathology courses. How he had loved learning to practice medicine from mentors such as a surgeon who taught him how to set bones and stitch wounds, and the importance of keeping the wounds clean.

This surgeon had guided him in the care of a young woman with a leg fracture at a hospital in downtown Chicago. The young woman insisted she had fallen while walking down a flight of stairs in the building where she lived, but Doctor Harvey had doubts about the story. The bruises on her face, neck, and arms did not seem to him likely to occur from a fall down stairs. The nurses at the hospital told him they had seen the young woman before with similar bruises. Each time the woman had been seen she told of an accident and declined offers to find a safe place to stay. She had remained in the hospital for two days after Doctor Harvey set the fracture. But when she left with her leg in a cast, she was accompanied by a man who seemed quite unsympathetic and scolded her for leaving him alone.

One nurse had told Doctor Harvey, "She'll be back, if she lives through the next beating. We can't convince her to leave him because she sees no alternative." This had troubled Doctor Harvey ever since.

After his internship he had joined the established medical practice of physician in a town about a two-hour train ride northwest of Chicago. Soon he was seeing more than ten patients daily, including railroad workers who were based there. His physician partner had a contract with the Chicago, Milwaukee, St. Paul Railroad Company, known by many as the Milwaukee Road, to provide medical care to company workers. Doctor Harvey had seen some of these workers now and then when his partner was not available.

One day at the medical office he had been introduced to Marie, a lovely young woman whose sparkling eyes entranced him and whose lilting voice enticed him to ask her one question after another so he could hear the voice again and again. Marie had brought a sack lunch to her sister, who was an office assistant at the medical practice. She had continued to bring lunches for her sister and to take lunchtime walks with Doctor Harvey. Before long Marie and Doctor Harvey were together for picnics, evening walks, and concerts at the town park; by Easter 1915 they were having dinner with Marie's family. That summer he had asked her to marry him. When she said yes his heart was pounding. Never before had he felt more anticipation, more optimism for the future.

They were married in July. In December, when she told him she had missed her period for the second consecutive month, he held her tightly and felt an overwhelming sense of wonder and expectation. During the winter, as Marie became more obviously pregnant, they were cheerful, their interactions loving, and their talk all about life with a child. But in June she had begun complaining of severe headaches; her blood pressure had climbed, her kidneys produced little urine, and she had been admitted severely ill to the hospital.

He had cancelled all patient appointments in order to sit at her bedside day and night for three days. She became less and less responsive. Then the obstetrician caring for her told him little more could be done; he should pray and hope for the best. He was dazed. How could this be? How could he know so little, do so little? How could medicine have nothing more to offer? Marie died on the fourth day in the hospital. The boy fetus, eight months in gestation, also died.

Doctor Harvey was devastated. The funeral was a blur. He began seeing patients again at the medical practice, but he had to force himself to get out of bed each morning, to concentrate on stories his patients shared about their own illnesses. He had no appetite, no energy. He knew he was deep in grief. He wanted to mourn somewhere else, someplace where everything he saw did not remind him of Marie.

His physician partner had been supportive but increasingly concerned as the summer weeks of 1916 went by. He sensed Doctor Harvey wanted to be somewhere else. In mid-November he said, "Kelly, I'm going to mention something to you and I don't want you to feel I am encouraging you to take any action. I'm just sharing some information."

Doctor Harvey looked at his partner for a minute then replied, "All right, although your tone sounds ominous."

"Well," said his partner, "a colleague of mine from medical school days has been in practice in Montana for a number of years. He's happy there, even served as mayor of the small town for a time. He recently joined the Army Medical Corps and the Army may be sending him to a military hospital assignment. Seems some think we might get more involved in that European war before long.

"Now here's what I want to mention to you. My colleague is looking for a physician who could take over his practice for a while. There's no way to know how long the Army might keep him busy, but he tells me the town could use another physician in any event, so even after he returns there'll be plenty of medicine to practice."

Doctor Harvey was intrigued by this situation. He imagined practicing in a new place without making a long-term commitment—yet still have the possibility of establishing his own practice in time.

"So you are not encouraging me to take any action, but you are just sharing this information with me?"

His partner replied, "Yes, although I think you would be an excellent candidate to do something like this. And it might be good for you to spend some time away from here for a while. Of course you would always be welcome to return."

Doctor Harvey continued to imagine practicing in a new setting. Many questions came to his mind. *Were there other physicians in the town? Was there a hospital? Where was this town anyway?*

He responded, "Thank you for mentioning this. I'd like to learn more."

Now he was in Montana, placing a splint on a young boy's fractured leg. This young boy and many others in Forsyth, including workers for both the Milwaukee Road and the Northern Pacific Railroad companies, relied on him to diagnose and treat their ailments, ease their suffering, and share their aspirations while he continued to deal with his own deep loss. He was carrying on.

CHAPTER FOUR

April 17, 1917
Later Afternoon

"He needs rest now," said Doctor Harvey, looking first at the somnolent Raymond and then at Amanda Swensen. "I'd like to see him every day for a few days. If we had a hospital in Forsyth, I'd want him to stay there until I can be sure his wound is healing without signs of infection," he continued without mentioning that lockjaw or amputation remained possible outcomes of such a wound.

He concluded by asking, "Is there a place in town you and your sons can stay for a few days?"

"We need to get back to our homestead," she said. Her face was bloodless, pained by the dilemma she was confronting. "My husband is away. I have no way to reach him. We have animals to tend. I don't know whom we would stay with in town. I don't have money to stay at the hotel. I will need to care for Raymond."

Not wishing to be critical or confrontational but hoping to find a way for Raymond to remain in Forsyth at least a few days, Doctor Harvey asked, "Is there a telephone we could call to get a message to your husband? Or maybe we could contact a neighbor who would tend your animals?"

May added, "You would be welcome to stay at my house. It's too late now to travel back to your homestead in a wagon tonight anyway. I've got plenty for supper for all of us and I would enjoy some company. My husband is away tonight, too, at a railroad meeting in Portland. He's an engineer with Northern Pacific. Tomorrow you could think further about a place to stay for a few days."

"That is very kind of you," said Amanda. "It would be best not to drive the wagon home in the dark. I would appreciate staying with you tonight."

Turning to Doctor Harvey she went on, "My husband is helping build a house down by Ashland but I don't know where the nearest telephone would be. I'd rather not trouble our neighbors with our animals tonight. I think we'll return to the homestead tomorrow. Please show me what I need to do to care for my son's leg and what I need to watch for. I'll bring him back here if there is a need."

Doctor Harvey placed his hand on Amanda's shoulder. "You are a brave woman. Your sons are fortunate to have such a mother. May I ask about your home, and about how Raymond broke his leg?"

"Of course," said Amanda, relieved to have a plan in place, even if not an optimal one. "Raymond is so rambunctious. He was running in the field near our house with Bingo, our dog. Bingo was barking and running back and forth in front of Raymond, as he often does to warn us when a rattlesnake is near. Raymond must have seen the snake. He turned quickly and began to run down the hill towards the house. I saw him fall and tumble off a rock ledge. He screamed then rolled further."

She paused. Her face had a pained look but she continued, "I left the clothes I was washing and ran to him. Oh my, those clothes are still in the wash water. When I got to Raymond his face was pale but he was breathing. Bingo licked his face and kept circling him, probably to make sure no snake was near. Raymond had fallen from that large rock and then rolled into the barbed wire fence."

She stopped for a moment. Tears were welling up in her eyes. "I knew his leg must be broken and there was blood on his pant leg. I knew I had to get him to town."

Doctor Harvey asked, "How did you get him into the wagon?"

Amanda took a deep breath and looked out the window into the distance. "I yelled at Axel to hitch Dan to the wagon. Dan is strong but gentle to handle. Axel did this quickly. I am so proud of him," she said while putting her arm around Axel and squeezing him to her side.

"While he hitched the horse and brought the wagon into the field, I moved Raymond away from the fence and put my shawl over him. Axel helped me lift Raymond onto the wagon bed. I was trying to be careful. I hope I didn't hurt him." Tears were now streaking down her face.

Doctor Harvey said, "You two did a terrific job. Your ability to get him out of the field in this way likely minimized the trauma that would have occurred if you had tried to carry or drag him to the house."

May handed Amanda a damp cloth, and she wiped her face. She continued, "When we got the wagon to the house, I hitched Stormy so we would have a two-horse team to pull the wagon all the way to town in case I could not find a neighbor with an automobile to use. My husband has our Overland down by Ashland. Once we got the wagon onto Reservation Creek Road, Axel drove the team as fast as he could, but that road is rough and rutted from the rains. I tried to comfort Raymond. His head was on my lap. Axel had thrown blankets into the wagon while I was hitching Stormy. Thank goodness for those blankets to keep Raymond warm."

She paused briefly before continuing, "As we came towards town we stopped at homes of neighbors with automobiles, but no one was there. By the time we made it to the intersection with River Valley Road and turned towards town, I decided to finish the trip in the wagon. That road was much better for driving a wagon than Reservation Creek Road had been."

Doctor Harvey asked, "How far is it from your homestead to town?"

"It is about twelve miles to town but it seemed to take forever. Raymond fell at about noon. I remember hearing a train's whistle as it headed west between town and Howard Junction. Do you recall what time it was when we arrived?"

Doctor Harvey said, "You came about two o'clock, only a few minutes after the afternoon train left the station. So you have done enough work for today. It's time for you and Axel to rest and have a good meal. May will see to that. I will go with you to get Raymond into bed for the night. He may be able to eat some soft food or liquid, but he won't be eating much tonight."

May asked Axel to come with her to get her automobile ready to take Raymond to her house.

Axel said, "But I need to remove the harness and brush Dan and Stormy."

"No need to worry about that," said May. "The men at the livery already wiped them down and brushed them. They have had hay and grain and lots of water, too. You can get them tomorrow."

After May and Axel left the office, Doctor Harvey said to Amanda, "I meant it when I said you are a very brave woman."

He continued, "I hope you don't mind me asking, are you pregnant?"

Amanda was surprised at first by the question, but replied, "Yes, I am. Does it show already?"

Doctor Harvey didn't mention he had suspected a pregnancy when her abdomen pressed against his hip while they moved Raymond from the wagon. Instead he said, "Just a physician's intuition, I guess. I'd like to talk with you more tomorrow about your home and tell you some of the things you'll need to do to care for Raymond during the next several days. Right now though let's get you and your boys to May's house."

He prepared a bedpan and other items to take to May's house. When May and Axel returned, Doctor Harvey and Axel carried Raymond from the office, down one flight of stairs, and out to May's Ford. Doctor Harvey and Axel placed Raymond in the front seat next to his mother, and May drove them the short four blocks to her home.

After making Raymond as comfortable as possible in a bedroom and watching him eat a small portion of mashed potatoes and drink two large glasses of water, Doctor Harvey gave him a dose of opium solution by mouth. This would allow the boy to sleep through the night without pain. He left the bedpan beside the bed and told Amanda her son should not get out of bed even to go to the bathroom.

From May's house he walked back to his room at the Alexander Hotel. When he had first come to Forsyth, he had planned to find an apartment or maybe a house. But since the day he arrived, the medical practice was so busy that little time remained for such a search.

His room included a bathroom with running water and a flush toilet. The hotel manager had agreed to place a small icebox and electric hotplate in one corner of the sitting room. This allowed him to prepare some meals, primarily breakfast, in his room. There was also a telephone on which he received calls at all hours. Long days spent in his office left only enough time to eat, sleep, and sometimes read the *Journal of the American Medical Association* and the *Boston Medical and Surgical Journal,* which came to him weekly on the Milwaukee Road mail car.

When he had time to relax he found himself thinking of Marie and how helpless he had felt during her illness. What more could he have done? He wondered if it was his own ignorance or just huge gaps in medical science responsible for the loss of Marie and their unborn child. He would sit motionless, staring out the window when these thoughts and doubts filled his mind. Then he would begin sipping the Flying U Rye Whiskey he'd bought from the Choisser liquor store on Ninth near the hotel. The next morning when he awoke, another empty bottle would be sitting on his desk.

CHAPTER FIVE

April 18, 1917

"Were you able to get some sleep?" Doctor Harvey asked Amanda the following morning. She did not appear rested.

May slid her arm around Amanda's waist and said, "She sat with Raymond most of the night but he slept quietly. He is awake now. He ate some scrambled eggs earlier."

Looking at Amanda, Doctor Harvey repeated his advice from the previous day, "I think it would be best if you stayed in town for a few more days."

"We can't. We need to get back to the homestead," said Amanda. "What do I need to do to care for Raymond?"

"You are a stubborn woman," he said almost affectionately.

Amanda did not reply, but the look on her face confirmed she took pride in this observation.

He then explained the essential steps for wound care, the importance of keeping Raymond's right leg immobile, and the need to contact him as soon as possible if the boy developed a fever or signs of inflammation around the wound. As he sometimes did to stress the importance of information given to his patients, he shared some history. The advice he gave was described centuries ago by Roman medical writer Celsus, who used the Latin words *rubor, tumor, calor,* and *dolor* for the redness, swelling, heat, and pain characteristic of the inflammation Doctor Harvey was concerned about. He handed a paper to Amanda. On it he had written the instructions for Raymond's care.

He concluded by saying, "Please bring Raymond to my office five days from now in any event. I would like to assess the wound healing then and make plans to replace the splint with a cast. He won't be able to bear weight on that leg for five or six months."

The expression on Amanda's face mixed resolve with hesitation. She said simply, "Thank you."

She turned to Axel. "Go to the stable and get Dan and Stormy into harness and hitched to the wagon. Ask the stable owner how much we owe for care of our horses. We've got a long trip to make so we should start soon."

"Let me suggest another way to get Raymond home," said Doctor Harvey. "This morning I called Mr. Matte, who lives out in your direction on Reservation Creek Road. He and one of his sons plan to come to town to get some supplies at the mercantile store. He will need a wagon to carry the supplies so he intended to come to town with horses and a wagon. I asked him if he'd consider driving his automobile to town instead and then taking you and your boys back to your homestead in the auto. His son could load the supplies into your wagon, drive the wagon to the Matte ranch, and then bring the empty wagon back to your homestead. He would get his supplies, you would get your wagon and horses, and Raymond would get home without bouncing around in the wagon for twelve miles."

Amanda looked surprised but very appreciative of this idea and said, "Are you sure Mr. Matte was planning to come to town today? I don't want to cause him trouble."

"Well," said Doctor Harvey, "he probably could have waited a little longer to get the supplies but he does need them. He is willing to drive his automobile to town and take you and your boys back to your homestead. I told him I'd call again after I discussed this plan with you."

"You are all so kind," said Amanda, looking first at May and then at Doctor Harvey. "That plan sounds like a good one for us."

"I will call Mr. Matte. I expect he'll be here within an hour," he said.

May asked, "Would you like to have a cup of coffee before you see patients today? The first appointment is not scheduled until 11:00 a.m."

"I'd love a cup of coffee," he said. "May I use your telephone to call Mr. Matte?"

After the telephone call he asked Amanda, "Maybe I can learn a little more about your homestead and how you decided to come to this area?"

Specifying the most common land size for homesteads sponsored by the 1909 Homestead Law, he asked, "Are you working a half section?"

Amanda replied, "We have a half section plus eighty more acres we were able to file on. Charles, my husband, had the well dug. It provides water year round. Our home is about a half mile from Reservation Creek Road. We have glass windows. We brought them from Iowa when we moved here in 1914. Charles is a carpenter. He built the house with those windows in mind. We have four rooms, five if you count the kitchen and living area as two, although they are really in one large room together. It is very comfortable. Our stove keeps us warm during the winter. I play my piano. Charles had it shipped from Iowa, too. And he plays fiddle. Sometimes we sing while he and I play. Music is a part of our family. Sometimes neighbors come on Sundays and we all sing and dance."

"Does Axel go to school?" asked May.

"Oh yes," replied Amanda. "He walks to the Ash Grove School. Miss Martens is a wonderful teacher. We need to make different arrangements in the autumn because Axel will be in the sixth grade, so he'll need to get to Howard School."

Doctor Harvey said, "You mentioned your husband is a carpenter. That is a special skill."

Amanda's face brightened as she replied, "He is very skilled. He is able to make extra money by helping build homes. He has helped our neighbors and is helping another Iowa family now down by Ashland."

"What animals do you have?" he asked.

"A milk cow, a young steer, a sow pig, some chickens, and Bingo, our dog," replied Amanda. "They will all be happy to see us come home, especially the milk cow. Her udder will be ready to burst. And all need feed and water."

"Well, I'd best go to my office now," said Doctor Harvey. "Remember to contact me right away if Raymond develops a fever or the skin around the wound becomes red and swollen. Mr. Matte will be here soon so you and your sons can get back to your homestead."

He turned to May. "There is no hurry for you to get to the office this morning. Just come when you can."

"Thank you again, both of you, for all you have done," said Amanda as he opened the door to leave.

"You are surely welcome," he said and then left the house.

When May arrived at the office about an hour later, she told Doctor Harvey how Mr. Matte—a large, burly man—had carried Raymond so carefully to his automobile. And how Amanda, Axel, and Raymond had each thanked her again before the auto moved away.

The patients he saw that afternoon came with diseases and conditions of the type he had grown accustomed to seeing in this community. One patient, a Milwaukee Road lineman aged twenty-seven, came to have his bandaged right hand examined. Doctor Harvey had applied the bandage the previous week after cleaning and stitching a laceration on the man's palm and repairing the stump of a thumb that remained after the hand was caught between ends of two rails during an attempt to repair a railroad track. The wound edges were red but not swollen. Doctor Harvey cleansed the area and applied a new bandage hoping the man would escape osteomyelitis, a complication unfortunately common in injuries of this type.

As Doctor Harvey offered instructions for further wound care, the man mentioned another problem, "Doc, I'm having pain when I pee."

Doctor Harvey asked a series of questions, "When did you first notice this pain?"

"A few days ago," he said.

"How often does it occur?"

"Each time I take a piss," he replied.

"Does your urine have its usual color?"

"It's cloudy, and it smells funny," he reported.

"With whom have you had sex during the past month?"

"I'm not married, no steady partner, but I had sex with prostitutes over in Miles City more than once," the man said.

"Drop your drawers and I'll take a look," said Doctor Harvey. He saw immediately a yellowish discharge from the man's penis and took a sample to stain and examine with his nearby microscope. Within a few minutes he provided a diagnosis and treatment.

"I suspect you know already you have a case of the clap," he announced. "I'm going to infuse a solution into your urethra and keep it in place for a few minutes. Then I'll rinse out the solution with some warm salt water."

"You mean you are going to put something into my pee hole?" queried the worried man.

"Yes," said Doctor Harvey. "That's the treatment for gonorrhea. It is recommended daily for up to four weeks. I'll provide treatments here during the next week and prepare you to treat yourself at home after that."

Doctor Harvey knew Army physicians were treating tens of thousands of cases of gonorrhea with the same silver-containing solution, protargol, that he was recommending to this man. The Army was prescribing daily irrigation for three months, but he doubted the chance this railroad lineman would continue such a regimen more than three or four weeks. Even if the treatment was successful, he also suspected that despite his advice the man would likely become reinfected from other partners.

"I need to take a blood sample, too," he told the lineman. "I'll send it to a laboratory in Helena to be tested for syphilis. We will talk more when I have the results," he continued. He knew if the laboratory found antibodies against syphilis in this blood that a separate, extensive treatment regimen would be needed. He would cross that bridge with this man if necessary.

Another patient, a woman aged sixty-eight, had high blood pressure and large, swollen ankles. She told of difficulty breathing. After examining her, he concluded her heart was slowly failing to function. She had been told by another physician she had dropsy, and Doctor Harvey concurred with the diagnosis although he told the woman her condition could also be called heart failure. He gave her a prescription for digitalis and told her it would help her heart function. She could fill the prescription at the pharmacy in this building right below his office. He also recommended a salt-restricted diet and asked her to see May to schedule another visit in two weeks so he could assess how this dose of digitalis was working.

Other patients he saw that afternoon included a man with tuberculosis who was continuing to lose weight, a woman with occasional urine incontinence who wanted to discuss use of a pessary mentioned to her by a friend, and a young mother whose baby kept crying and refusing to breast feed. He saw a half dozen other patients as well.

Doctor Harvey found his work stimulating, and enjoyed being challenged to solve the wide variety of problems. He had come to learn that each day's ailments were completely different than the next. He wondered if medical science might one day be equipped to help with all these issues; he knew that in many cases there was only so much physicians could do.

Around 5:00 p.m. May came into his office area in the examination room. "That was the last appointment for today," she said. "I have filed the records, receipts, and the IOUs. Some patients paid cash, some pledged to pay later, one wondered if you would barter your services for eggs or cheese, and of course the railroad workers' visits are paid by the contracts with Milwaukee Road and Northern Pacific. I have the cash payments in an envelope in the safe. I'll take it to the bank on Friday."

He had almost finished recording notes about the patients he had seen. He asked, "What did you tell the patient who wanted to barter for eggs or cheese?"

"I told her I would need to discuss that with you but for the time being the amount due would stay on our books," said May.

"I'll give some thought to bartering. For now, however, keeping track of the amount due seems reasonable," he replied.

He continued, "Thank you for the great work you do, and especially for your help with Amanda Swensen. I want to add some money to your pay this month to help with some of the expenses you incurred because of your kindness."

"No extra pay, please. I was happy to help and so were the folks at the livery. We know she would do the same for us if the shoe were on the other foot," replied May. "If we had a hospital in town, would you have admitted Raymond as you said to Amanda?"

"Yes, and she and Axel could have stayed with him. It would have been dangerous for them all, especially Raymond, to try to get home in a wagon so late in the day. Your kindness allowed them to avoid that danger. If a hospital were available, Raymond should have stayed for several days even after his mother and Axel had returned to the homestead," he responded.

May continued, "I do hope the commissioners decide to build a hospital. It's not only situations like Raymond's. Many patients who travel to Billings or Miles City could have hospital care here instead."

"The commissioners are dealing with many issues, but I will encourage them to find a way to have a hospital built in Forsyth. It would be possible to attract a nurse or two to live here as well when full-time work at a hospital was available," said Doctor Harvey, looking beyond May as if staring into the future.

"Thank you again," he continued. "It is a beautiful evening for your walk home. I'm going to the café for a bite to eat. I might just see a commissioner while I am there."

May put on her gray Butterick coat with the collar draping over her shoulders. She held her purse in the crook of her arm as she opened the office door.

"I really enjoy working here," she said, perhaps wondering how her job might be affected if more nurses moved to town.

A few minutes later Doctor Harvey left the office and walked a half block to the café.

"Good evening, Alice," he said to the plump, middle-aged woman who was often his waitress at the café—which, aside from the saloons and the general mercantile store, had more visitors on most days than did other gathering places in town. "Any chance you are serving meatloaf tonight?"

"Why Doctor Harvey, of course we have your favorite dish. Every night we hope you come and every night you do come you order meatloaf so we try always to have it," said Alice with a distinct Irish lilt. Doctor Harvey didn't eat at the café every night, but he had eaten there several times each week since he arrived in town.

"Please have a seat," she said as she gestured toward a small table with two chairs near a window, where he often sat. "May I hang your coat while you are eating?"

He nodded, handed his coat to Alice, and sat down. He had glanced around the room while talking with Alice. Although he saw no county commissioners, he noticed the bank cashier and a rancher sitting at a table near his.

"Good evening, gentlemen," he said.

The banker responded with a rousing, "Evening, Doctor. Good to see you have some time to enjoy a meal. Seems like our town has more than enough maladies to keep you busy round the clock. You are welcome to join us if you like, but we are just finishing so we may be leaving by the time your food is served."

"I appreciate the offer but I don't want to keep you from your families," replied Doctor Harvey. Alice arrived with a place setting and a cup of hot coffee; there was no need to ask about cream since she knew he always drank his coffee black.

"Would you like your potatoes mashed or boiled tonight?" she said, asking about the one part of his meal that varied from visit to visit.

"Mashed potatoes and lots of butter," he said. Then he listened while Alice provided her always optimistic observations about how the town was growing; how more businesses would open and thrive in town; how electricity and telephone connections had made life easier for town dwellers and that these amenities would reach ranches and homesteads throughout the county in time; how more teachers would be needed; how automobiles had mostly replaced horses and wagons; and more until she excused herself to check on diners at another table.

While Alice had been talking, Doctor Harvey couldn't help overhearing some of the conversation between the banker and the rancher. Both were convinced German people living in Rosebud County and elsewhere in Montana must be watched carefully. They felt espionage and even sabotage might already be occurring by what they were calling "pawns of the Kaiser" right here in Montana. Names mentioned in the conversation included Judge Crum, the district judge for this area, and the rancher Mr. Mueller.

To Doctor Harvey these concerns seemed over-dramatized, quite unlikely to be occurring, and even less likely to pose a real threat to the U.S. war effort. However, part of the discussion between the banker and rancher particularly concerned him.

The banker had said, "I think we can make folks like Mueller pay a heavy price for disloyalty. The bank note for the wheat seed he purchased will be due soon. He may not be able to make good on that note and I don't think the bank is inclined to offer extensions to traitors."

To this the rancher had added, "By all rights those acres should belong to real Americans anyway."

Doctor Harvey recognized the toxic nature of these allegations and proposed remedies. When the banker and rancher stood to leave, he nodded his head in their direction and said, "Good evening."

Alice arrived with a nicely displayed plate full of meatloaf and steaming-hot mashed potatoes with a pool of melted butter. After eating this and a piece of hot apple pie, he put a dollar and a half on the table and thanked Alice for another delicious meal. Then he walked across Ninth Avenue to the Alexander Hotel and to his room.

CHAPTER SIX

June 6, 1917

May was arranging flowers in a vase on her desk in the office entry area. She had picked these early-June blooms from her beloved flower garden that morning. The fragrance of the bell-shaped white, peach, and orange hyacinths was an unmistakable reminder of spring turning to summer. Red and pale-yellow tulips, purple and white bicolored irises, and yellow daffodils added to the explosion of colors in the vase.

The fragrance and the colors made Doctor Harvey think of Marie and how she had loved flowers. He also thought of reports from Europe about the endless battle there, the numbers of flowers loved ones would be placing on graves once the bloodletting subsided, the young men who would not live to be fathers.

"How many railroad workers are scheduled today?" he asked May, knowing a crew change had occurred and members of one crew would have a layover in town. For some workers a layover in a town where the company had contracted with a physician was the only opportunity for medical care. Thus visits for a work-related injury or condition were sometimes extended for evaluation of additional medical issues.

Doctor Harvey asked, "Who else is on the schedule?"

"Three railroad workers will be coming this morning, and Frances Olson, the county school superintendent, wants to talk with you at noon," replied May.

"I'll be glad to talk with her. Interesting she is coming here," remarked Doctor Harvey.

The office door opened and a portly man who appeared to be at least fifty years old entered. He removed his wool cap, but when he slipped off his hip-length jacket he leaned slightly to his left as if to avoid moving his right side. May greeted him and motioned toward Doctor Harvey.

"Please come right in," said Doctor Harvey.

After both men were in the examination room he continued, "What brings you for medical attention today?"

The man replied with a British accent, "I keep having pains right here." He pointed to his right lower abdomen and groin area.

"When did you begin feeling this pain?" asked Doctor Harvey.

"About three weeks ago in Illinois," he said. "I supervise a crew of linemen for the Milwaukee Road. We were repairing track outside Rockford. I started to pick up a rail and darned if I didn't trip and fall beside the track. I felt the pain when I stood up."

"Did you seek medical attention then?" asked Doctor Harvey.

"I saw a doctor the next day. He told me I had a hernia and might need surgery to fix it," replied the railroad worker. "But I asked that doctor if there was some other way to fix this. He said I could try using a truss but I might need surgery eventually to control the pain. So I've been wearing a truss. The pain keeps coming and going."

Doctor Harvey asked several questions about the pain in order to learn it was right-sided, intermittent, and associated with movement. He asked the railroad worker to drop his drawers. The worker's truss was white, although it would be much whiter if washed, and consisted of a waistband and straps extending from front to back on either side of the worker's scrotum.

He told the worker he needed to examine his lower abdomen. He saw a mass protruding from the right inguinal area. He palpated the mass and asked the worker to cough. The bulge protruded further.

The worker said, "I feel the pain now, Doc."

The remainder of the physical exam was unremarkable. He asked the worker to reposition the truss and get dressed.

He said, "You need to have surgery before this gets worse. Right now the hernia bulge is just part of the sac from the abdominal cavity. It's called an omentum. But if part of the intestine drops into the hernia area, it could get stuck. We call that incarcerated. If the intestine lost its blood supply, emergency surgery would be necessary. It would be better to schedule surgery now rather than chance an emergency."

"Could you do the surgery here?" asked the worker.

"If there was an emergency I could reduce the hernia here," he replied. "However, I recommend you see a surgeon, and there is a good one in Miles City. If you agree I'll call him to schedule an appointment. I think you should not return to work until you have had the surgical repair."

"Well, I guess I'd better have the surgery," said the worker. "Please go ahead and contact the surgeon to see when I could get this done."

"Could you get to Miles City sometime this week?" asked Doctor Harvey.

The man indicated he could take the train any day.

"I will call and schedule a time. I will also prepare a letter you can use to arrange some work time off for the surgery and recovery," he said. "If you come back later this morning, my assistant, May, will have the letter and more information about seeing the surgeon."

He walked with the worker into the office entry area. He told May this worker would return for more information later and asked her to prepare a medical leave letter for him to complete and sign.

Before seeing the next patient, he called the Miles City surgeon's office and left a message with the office assistant there. He requested a return call to confirm a time when this patient could be seen and when an inguinal hernia repair could be done.

May said, "The next railroad worker is here. He does not look well."

Doctor Harvey replied, "Please ask him to come in."

The young man was about five feet ten inches in height and very thin. Doctor Harvey imagined this man might have trouble staying upright if he were outside during a stiff Montana windstorm. Like the previous worker this man removed a wool cap and a hip length jacket, but under the jacket he wore a woolen pullover sweater. Doctor Harvey thought it unusual to wear such a heavy sweater on a sunny June day with only a mild wind blowing.

"Please have a seat," said Doctor Harvey. "What brings you for medical attention today?"

The young man sat. His eyes were sunken and his thoughts seemed to be elsewhere.

"I'm afraid I cannot work any longer. I have no energy," he said.

Doctor Harvey guessed this man was chronically ill and might have received some medical attention previously. He responded, "Tell me a little more about yourself. Do you see another physician, too?"

"Oh yes," said the man. "I have a doctor back home in Rockford. About six or eight months ago he told me I have diabetes. I've been trying to follow his advice but I just keep feeling weaker and weaker. I want to know if there is anything I can do to get over this."

Doctor Harvey replied, "I'll double check to confirm the diagnosis, but if you have diabetes the treatment options are limited. There is no known cure. What treatment are you using now?"

The young man looked at him for a moment then said, "I'm starving. That's what the doctor advised me to do. But it is hard to eat so little when I am hungry and have no energy for work. I still pee frequently and I'm always thirsty."

Doctor Harvey was aware of this type of treatment for diabetes. He had learned about it during his training at Northwestern. American doctors in Boston were leading advocates of severe calorie-restricted diets. They advised repeated fasting and prolonged undernourishment. They knew this was not a cure but wanted to relieve symptoms caused by too much sugar, glucose, in the blood. The goal of this treatment was to extend a patient's life. However, the extent to which a starvation diet achieved this goal was not clear to Doctor Harvey. He leaned toward an alternate treatment he had also learned at Northwestern.

He asked, "Before you began limiting your food intake so strictly, were there times you would lose consciousness?"

"I did, more than once," replied the man. "That's when my doctor told me to fast and expect to lose much of my weight."

Doctor Harvey asked the young man to urinate into a container. The urine smelled sweet like syrup. He tested it and found a very high level of sugar. Then he reviewed information about diabetes with the patient.

"I'm sure you know diabetes leads to too much sugar building up in your blood. This causes the thirst you have. Your kidneys rid your body of some of the sugar and this causes your frequent urination. When the blood sugar level gets very high, it is called hyperglycemia and can cause loss of consciousness. This can be life threatening. The severely restricted diet is one way to try to avoid this crisis."

He paused briefly and continued, "There is an alternate approach for diet treatment for diabetes. Instead of severely restricting the entire diet, the alternate approach restricts foods containing carbohydrates. The body converts carbohydrates to sugars. This alternate approach emphasizes meats in the diet, so it is sometimes called an animal diet. With this diet you would gain some weight back. You might not need to wear such a heavy sweater during the summer, although you would probably still have frequent urination and bouts of thirst. It is not a cure, just an alternate approach."

The young man seemed more animated when he replied, possibly ascribing more hope to the alternate approach than Doctor Harvey had intended. He said, "I would like to try the alternate approach. If I could gain some weight I could keep working."

Doctor Harvey replied cautiously, "I can't promise the animal diet would increase your energy level, although it is likely you would gain some weight. I will give you information about this diet so you could begin trying it. I encourage you to discuss this with your doctor when you get back to Rockford, too."

Doctor Harvey then gave his patient written information describing the low-carbohydrate diet many physicians were recommending. He did not tell the young man to return to work. Instead he advised him to wait until he gained some weight. At that time a decision regarding readiness and safety for work could be considered. He was not optimistic about this patient working again in the near future but saw no reason to share his doubts today.

The polite young man said, "Thank you, Doctor. I will try this diet." He donned his jacket, carried his cap, and also said thank you to May as he departed.

The third railroad worker to visit was the lineman with gonorrhea Doctor Harvey had seen in April. Doctor Harvey asked, "Have you been able to continue treating yourself with the urethral infusions each day? The recommended duration for this treatment is six weeks and it has been five since your treatment began."

The lineman replied, "Well, Doc, I kept it up until this week, but it is a shit load of trouble to keep doing this."

"Are you having pain or burning when you urinate? Has your urine been cloudy, or have you seen blood in your urine?" asked Doctor Harvey.

"No," said the lineman. "I'm back to normal, close as I can tell. And I sure don't like that treatment."

Doctor Harvey thought for a minute. He suspected this man would not continue the urethral infusions even if recommended to do so. He also knew the regimen had not been convincingly documented to be effective.

He said, "Since your symptoms have cleared it is reasonable to discontinue the treatment after five weeks. Also, your blood test for syphilis was negative so no additional therapy is needed for that, at least at this time."

The lineman, clearly relieved by learning the treatment had ended, responded, "I appreciate your help. Guess I should be more careful about the houses I choose."

Doctor Harvey knew this man would continue visiting bordellos in the towns where he worked, so he advised, "If you want to lessen the chance of more bouts with clap, or with syphilis, you should wear protection regardless of the house you choose. This will help protect the women you do business with, too. They are supporting themselves and often others, so protection makes sense all around."

The lineman frowned but said nothing more. He nodded in reluctant recognition as he walked out of the examination room.

Doctor Harvey spent a few minutes writing notes in his office records about patients he had seen so far during the morning and then saw more patients seeking help for a variety of ailments. The last of these left a little before noon.

May knocked lightly on the examination room door.

Doctor Harvey said, "Come in."

"Superintendent Olson is here now," she said.

"Please tell her I'll be ready in just a few minutes," he said, realizing how unusual it was for a superintendent to visit him at his office.

Doctor Harvey had come to Forsyth to support a medical practice while a local physician served in the Army Medical Corps. From the moment the United States entered the war in Europe, the duration of Doctor Harvey's agreement to practice here was no more defined than was the duration of the local physician's commitment to the Army. He had been too busy in his medical practice to think about the ambiguity of this. He appreciated the opportunity he had.

Before enlisting in the Army Medical Corps, the local physician had also served as the county health officer, a position Montana state law required commissioners in each county to designate. Doctor Harvey had agreed to fulfill this role, too. Perhaps a public health issue had prompted today's visit? Rather than guess further he opened the door of the examination room.

"Hello, Frances. Please come in. I am looking forward to talking with you," he greeted.

He turned to May and said, "Please enjoy a lunch break. I'll see you this afternoon when the next patient is scheduled."

While Frances Olson walked into the examination room and sat in a chair near Doctor Harvey's desk, May stepped closer to him and said in a low voice, "Mr. Mueller called a few minutes ago to ask if you would see his niece this afternoon. I told him you would. He plans to bring her at 4:30. That is the last scheduled appointment today."

He said, "Thanks. Enjoy your lunch."

Doctor Harvey took a seat at his desk in the examination room and said, "It is a special privilege to have you here. Would you like some water or coffee?"

She shook her head to indicate no. She was a short, neatly dressed woman whose posture and intense gaze gave her an aura of authority. She began, "As you know, some students, three I believe, were away from school with smallpox this spring. Other students exposed to those students continued to come to school even though they had not had smallpox vaccination. I just returned from a school superintendents' meeting in Helena. Doctor Cogswell of the State Board of Health talked with us there. He said smallpox cases in school-age children had been reported from several areas in the state.

"He urged us to be sure all students had been vaccinated against smallpox. The State Board of Health plans to establish a rule to require smallpox vaccination for students and to exclude those who have not been vaccinated. I learned from my colleagues at the meeting that some school districts have plans to enforce such a requirement."

Doctor Harvey said, "I haven't learned all I need to know yet as the county health officer. Has a requirement like this been considered already for Rosebud County schools?"

Frances replied, "No, not yet. That is what I want to discuss with you."

He thought for a moment about the smallpox cases he had seen since he arrived in this county. The cases included a nine-year-old girl, her younger brother, and a neighbor girl, eight years old, as well as brothers nine and twelve years old from a ranch southeast of town. He had made diagnoses for each of these unvaccinated children and told each family to keep ill children home and isolated from others for fourteen days after onset of illness. The families had agreed to do this, but keeping sick children isolated was not the biggest challenge for controlling spread of this disease.

The more difficult issue was trying to ensure that unvaccinated persons exposed to a smallpox case got vaccinated—or if they remained unvaccinated that they stayed home, so if they became ill they would not expose even more people.

He knew some parents were opposed to vaccination. Some of those opposed were vehemently against any government requirement, and some considered vaccination unnatural or against their religious beliefs. In medical school he had learned that some states had required smallpox vaccination for entry to public schools. He felt this requirement should be in place in Rosebud County, too. He had not fully realized unvaccinated students exposed to smallpox were remaining in school. This would certainly increase the spread of the disease.

"Of course I support the advice you received from Doctor Cogswell," he said. "It would be best to identify the unvaccinated students immediately and exclude them from school until they are vaccinated, or at least until fourteen days has passed since the last exposure to smallpox. This would be a quarantine measure. I will do whatever I can to help establish a vaccination and quarantine policy."

Frances said, "School is out for the summer, so there is time to work on this issue before school convenes in the autumn."

Doctor Harvey continued, "I need to review the quarantine policy not only for schools but also for other places public gatherings occur. For smallpox there is a vaccine to prevent the disease. However, for other communicable diseases, including whooping cough and scarlet fever, there is no vaccine. Isolation of patients with these diseases, along with quarantine of some persons exposed to these patients, is an important step we can take to prevent more disease. Perhaps we could prepare a policy recommendation and discuss it with the county commissioners before school reconvenes next autumn?"

She replied, "That would be an excellent approach."

Doctor Harvey said, "Yes, I'll prepare some text for quarantine and vaccination policies and get it to you within a few days. Thank you for coming today."

May entered the office as Frances Olson was leaving. She held the door open and said, "Very nice to see you."

"Nice to see you as well," Frances replied.

May looked at Doctor Harvey and asked curiously, "Was there enough time for your meeting?"

He replied, knowing May would like to learn the reason for the meeting. "We discussed some ideas related to quarantine and control of communicable diseases. We need to discuss some policy issues with the county commissioners. Someday medicine will know more about the causes and ways to control these diseases, but now we use control measures not so different from those used generations ago. At least we don't bleed patients these days. Well, most doctors don't!"

May seemed satisfied with that information. While removing her coat she said, "Your next patient should be here soon. Don't forget Mr. Mueller is bringing his niece this afternoon, too." Then she added, "Did you get any lunch? Should I get something for you?"

He said, "I can do without lunch today, but thank you for asking." He walked back into the examination room thinking more about vaccination and quarantine policies than about lunch.

The symptoms reported by patients during the afternoon were those he had become accustomed to assessing. One man told of coughing blood, weight loss, fever, and night sweats. Doctor Harvey suspected tuberculosis and collected sputum for laboratory examination.

A woman reported she had trouble breathing and swollen ankles. He diagnosed heart failure and talked with her about the foxglove flower and a drug called digitalis. Other patients had a variety of pains, sprains, and a drain problem as one man described his difficulty urinating. All in all it was a typical afternoon in a rural doctor's medical practice.

At 4:30 he heard May talking with a man whose strong German accent and use of German words in otherwise English sentences made it easy for him to guess Herman Mueller had arrived. He stepped from the examination room into the entry room and said, "Guten Tag Herr Mueller."

"Guten Tag," came a reply.

"Ich habe…I brought my niece to see you. She ist nicht eating, nicht sleeping," he began to list problems he had perceived.

Doctor Harvey interrupted as politely as he could, not wanting the young woman to feel uncomfortable while her uncle recited his reasons for her visit today. He said, "I have not had the pleasure to meet your niece."

Herman had stopped talking but quickly resumed, "This is Gerde, meine Nichte. She has lived with us vier Jahre. Meine Schwester sent her here in May 1914. After meine Schwager died in 1913, we planned for meine Schwester and her drei Kinder to come to live with us. She sent Gerde first but the terrible war began. She and her other children have not been able to come."

While he listened Doctor Harvey was observing the young woman who appeared very meek and shy and whose gaze was downward. He interrupted again to say, "Hello, Gerde."

He motioned toward the examination room and continued, "Perhaps you would like to come into this room to talk?"

He then looked at Herman and asked, "Would you like some coffee or water?"

He asked May, "Would you please get Mr. Mueller something to drink?"

"Yes. May I get you some coffee?" May asked while Gerde stepped into the examination room and Doctor Harvey closed the door.

"Please have a seat," he said while gesturing to a chair by his desk.

He remained struck by how quiet and shy she was. He asked, "Do you speak English? Sprechen Sie English?"

"I speak some English, ja," she replied as she sat in the chair.

He realized some help with German-English translation might be necessary in order to determine the reason for this visit. However, he had sensed the young girl was not comfortable when her uncle was telling her story for her. Thus he was not inclined to ask Herman to help interpret her statements at this time. Instead he decided to proceed.

"How old are you?" he asked.

"Ich bin achtzehn Jahre…eighteen years old," she replied.

"What is the reason you came today?" he asked.

She looked puzzled by this question but replied, "Mein Onkel brought me."

He rephrased the question, "Why do you need to see a physician? What problem are you having?"

She again looked puzzled and said, "I do not need a physician. Mein Onkel brought me here."

He rethought his approach to this shy, very attractive young woman. She had beautiful facial features, fair skin, high forehead, small nose, high cheekbones, and wide-set eyes. When she established eye contact, he sensed sadness in her medium-brown eyes. She sat very straight in the chair, hands clasped together in her lap. He asked, "Is there anything you want to talk about? Is there something I might be able to help with?"

She no longer looked puzzled. She appeared to be thinking about what to say or, perhaps, whether to say anything. After a long pause she said, almost too softly for him to hear, "Mein Onkel treats me well. I know he wants me to be happy. But I miss meine Mutter, seine Schwester. I miss meine Schwester und mein Bruder. I think of them always. I want to see them but I know I cannot. They are in Deutschland. I do not receive letters from them and cannot send letters." Tears welled up in her eyes. She looked downward again.

He reached across the desk to hand her a small towel. She took it and wiped the tears from her face. He said, "You must be very lonely. It is terrible this war has separated you from your mother and your family in Germany."

He paused before saying, "The war will not last forever."

She said, "I hope not. Every day seems to last forever. Ich bin eine burden for mein Onkel. He has too much burden." Her voice tailed off.

"The bank must be paid," she continued. "Die Nachbarn, the neighbors, no longer visit." Her voice tailed off again.

"Tell me about the neighbors," he said.

"When I first came we had Abendessen with Nachbarn each Sonntag. It was freudig, joyful. I talked with other Mädchen. Now we never see them. When mein Onkel comes to town he is called a Kraut lover, a traitor. He is nicht ein Verräter. He loves this country. We have no contact with Deutschland. I wish we could. I miss meine Mutter," she said softly.

"Your uncle said you were not eating and not sleeping," he said.

"I eat a little but I am not hungry. I do not schlafen when I go to bed so I get up and sit in a chair by the window until I einschlafen," she replied.

He felt confident she was depressed and opted not to take a more thorough medical history or conduct a physical examination at this time. He said, "I would like to give you some medication to help you sleep and also set a time for another office visit. Then you could tell me more about yourself and if the medication helped."

She did not reply, but the look on her face made him think she was willing to try some medication. He wrote a prescription for tincture of opium and handed it to her.

"Let's go see your uncle and May," he said.

When they returned to the entry room he said to Herman, "I think some medication will help Gerde sleep better. I have given her a prescription you can take to the pharmacy. She should take a teaspoon of the liquid at night just before going to bed."

To May he said, "Please schedule another office visit in two weeks."

Looking at Gerde he said, "Would that be acceptable to you?"

Gerde nodded in agreement. May suggested a date to which Herman agreed. Then he and Gerde departed.

"She seems like a very nice young lady," said May. "Rather quiet, but very nice."

"Quiet and thoughtful," he replied. "Unless other patients are scheduled we might as well go home. I'm ready for some supper and I'll bet you are, too."

May said, "One more thing. The Miles City surgeon called. A time for surgery later this week has been set. I told the railroad crew boss. He said he'd be there."

Doctor Harvey walked from the office to his room at the hotel. He took items from the icebox, sliced a bread loaf, and began eating. He thought about language to use in a vaccination and quarantine policy, the situation Herman Mueller and his family were experiencing, and Gerde's loneliness. The latter made him think of his own loneliness; how he missed Marie. He poured a glass of whiskey and sipped as he ate.

CHAPTER SEVEN

June 19, 1917

Doctor Harvey took a deep breath of the midmorning, early-summer air and held the corrugated grip on the walnut steering wheel of his 1916 Hudson Cabriolet. He looked through the heavy plate-glass windshield as he drove south on Reservation Creek Road. The Super Six Hudson had little trouble maintaining a speed of thirty miles per hour despite the not-yet-dried gumbo road surface from yesterday's rainstorm. When the journey began in Forsyth that morning, the tarmac road surface was dry and the automobile ride was smooth. After leaving town to the west on the crushed-gravel road through the Yellowstone River Valley, the ride had become bumpy but not uncomfortable on the eighteen-inch tires, which had improved automobile rides considerably since replacing the thinner, harder tires—like those used on the first automobiles. However, since turning south on Reservation Creek Road, the ride had been bone-jarring at times as he tried to avoid sliding off the gumbo-covered road into a ditch on either side.

He knew the automobile trip was quicker and more comfortable than travel in the horse-drawn wagons that some ranchers and homesteaders still used in this area. He wondered if rural roads like this would ever be built and maintained in a way equivalent to the increasingly comfortable roads in towns and cities.

"I appreciate the opportunity to accompany you on this trip," he said to the neatly dressed public health nurse who was sitting on the passenger side of the front seat. She was the only public health nurse available to conduct home visits to ranchers and homesteaders in a three-county area. She worked primarily with pregnant women, mothers, and children.

Doctor Harvey had contacted her in late April after Amanda Swensen had returned to her homestead with her son Raymond. He had asked the nurse to assess the status of Mrs. Swensen's pregnancy and review plans for delivery and care of a newborn. When Johanna, the nurse, let him know she had arranged to visit, he asked to go with her so he could assess how Raymond's leg was healing. He was also interested to learn more about the work of the public health nurse program and types of patients receiving services in this area.

She had driven to Forsyth that morning from her home in Miles City. When he offered to drive to the homestead, she readily accepted. During their time together so far they had discussed some cases she had seen in recent weeks as well as things she would like to see improved in the public health nurse program.

"I am very concerned about a young girl I visited last week at a ranch east of here off the Colstrip Road," said Johanna. "She just turned sixteen and she's pregnant, about three or four months. She lives with her mother, father, younger sister, and two brothers, one older and one younger than her. She is not married and would not tell me who the father of her baby is. I think she may have been violated and there may be ongoing molestation. She needs to be in a different living situation."

"My, oh my," said Doctor Harvey. "I do not know this family. Have her parents taken her to a physician? How are they helping her deal with this?"

"Neither her mother nor her father has been very helpful," said Johanna. "I'm afraid her father or older brother might be the father of her baby. She is in a terrible situation. The parents have not agreed to take her for medical attention yet, but I think they will if I keep encouraging them."

"Do you think they would take her to Doctor Lindeberg in Miles City? You probably work with her on some other cases already," he said. "She would be the best physician for this young woman to see. Whether the girl and her parents decide to terminate the pregnancy or she gives birth but gives up the baby, Doctor Lindeberg would be able to help. If they wanted the pregnancy and delivery to happen away from their ranch, she could help arrange living-in at the Florence Crittenton Home in Helena. She would almost certainly be the best physician for this case."

"I do work with Doctor Lindeberg. She is always very helpful and very caring," replied Johanna.

"If this pregnancy is the result of molestation, then the state children's services agency and law enforcement should also be involved," he observed.

"I think the parents are trying to look the other way, deny the presence of a problem, avoid involvement of legal and other agencies," said Johanna. "I hope to get the parents to take their daughter to a physician. I plan to see them again tomorrow."

Doctor Harvey didn't reply. He had been watching for a landmark Mrs. Swensen had described to him. A plateau on the left, shaped like a wolf's head in profile with an indentation serving as the eye, must be the landmark. The Swensen homestead's driveway was due west of the wolf's eye. He turned onto the even bumpier track, which wound back and forth as it climbed, descended, and climbed again for about half a mile. Finally they reached a crest, and he and Johanna looked down into a lovely small valley. He drove down the hill the last 200 yards and noted a house, a barn, a large garden area and low structures he guessed to be coverings for a root cellar and a well.

Beside the house a lilac bush was in bloom. He parked the Hudson in a flat area beside the home, a one-story wood-frame building with a peaked roof and the glass windows Amanda had described to him at May's house.

On the porch Amanda, now obviously pregnant, was standing with her arm around Raymond's shoulder. She said, "Hello. You made it."

He and Johanna stepped out of the automobile, said hello in return, and walked toward the porch. They drew the intense interest of the border collie—black with white patches—who bounced between the two of them, sniffing at shoes and legs, running ahead a few paces, then returning to examine the visitors further. Doctor Harvey held out his hand, palm up. Then he rubbed the top of the dog's head, gently at first but then more firmly.

He asked, "What is this handsome fella's name?"

Raymond, who had used crutches to descend two steps from the porch to the ground, replied, "His name is Bingo. He likes to have his head rubbed!"

Doctor Harvey was kneeling beside the dog and rubbing his head, neck, and back by the time Raymond arrived to join in petting the ecstatic canine. He said, "It's good to see you moving so well, Raymond. Maybe you and Bingo would show me around for a few minutes while your mother and the nurse have a chance to talk?"

To Amanda he said, "You may have met already. This is Johanna. She is very knowledgeable and can share some helpful information with you."

Amanda replied, "Yes. Very nice to see you."

She gestured to Johanna and said, "Please come in. Would you like some tea?" The two women went into the house.

Raymond began crutch-walking slowly to the right of the house, pointing to highlights of the homestead from the perspective of a seven-year-old boy for whom this was the world as he knew it. "There is the barn and the plow the horses pull and the chicken house and the outhouse," he said, pointing in turn to each.

Doctor Harvey was pleased to see how seemingly pain free the boy was. He planned to inspect the cast, which covered his leg from above the knee to below the ankle, before departing. He asked, "Do you feel any pain in your leg?"

"I feel some if I put my foot on the ground, but mom keeps telling me not to do that. She says I must use these crutches and not stand on my foot," said Raymond.

"I'm glad you are listening to your mother. You'll need to use the crutches for many more weeks. But by the time school starts again you should be able to walk without them," he said reassuringly.

At the crest of a plateau about 150 yards east of the barn, Axel rode into view on a large, brown horse. He carried a basket in one hand. When he got to the barn he said, "Hi, Doctor. I have some wild strawberries here. Mom thought you and the nurse might like to have a bowl of these." He handed the basket to Doctor Harvey and tied the horse to the rail on the hitching post beside the barn.

Doctor Harvey tasted one of the small, sweet strawberries and said, "Delicious. Thank you for picking these. Did you need to go far?"

"No," replied Axel. "There are lots of berries on the bench and they are ripening now. Dad grows watermelons up there, too, but coyotes sometimes get to the ripe melons before we do."

"Where does your land go from here?" asked Doctor Harvey.

Axel pointed first to the east and then to the north and south as he described the extent of the homestead. When he pointed west he said, "Our land ends just at the crest of the hill where the driveway comes down toward our house."

Doctor Harvey was puzzled and asked, "Does your land include the entire driveway over to Reservation Creek Road?"

"No. Dad and a neighbor have an agreement he calls a hand-shake agreement for us to use the path from that crest to the main road. It's not easy to get to the road in the winter or after heavy rain, but it would be harder if our driveway had to be farther south," Axel replied.

"Is your father away?" asked Doctor Harvey.

"He has our Overland down in Ashland where he is working again for a few days. When he gets back we'll probably be doing work on the driveway while the weather is good. Need to smooth some spots on the way to the main road," replied Axel. "That's the path I have used to get to Ash Grove School but next year I need to get to Howard School for sixth grade."

Raymond had listened quietly but he had been looking at the strawberries throughout the discussion. He interrupted, "Let's get these in to mom. She made some shortcake, too."

Doctor Harvey and Axel followed Raymond to the house, with Bingo darting between the three of them as they offered pats on the head and scratches behind the ears.

Inside the house Axel placed the basket of berries on the kitchen counter and Raymond eagerly asked, "Are we going to have strawberry shortcake?"

Amanda stopped talking with Johanna to say, "Yes, if our guests would like to try some."

She instructed the two boys to go wash their hands then turned to her guests. "Would you like to try some strawberries on shortcake? It will take only a few minutes."

Johanna said, "Please let me help remove the stems."

While the two women prepared the berries, Doctor Harvey glanced around the inside of the house. The main living area had only a table and four chairs separating the kitchen from a space where a cushioned chair and rocking chair sat on a rug covering part of the wood plank floor. In the kitchen was a stove with side-by-side compartments, one an oven and the other for wood burning. The compartments were topped by a cast-iron plate, on which sat a frying pan and a metal teapot. Also in the kitchen was a sink with running water and counters on either side. The view through the glass window above the sink was toward the barn.

Kerosene lamps were mounted on the walls. No electric items or telephone were present. He guessed the motor in the well house outside must be battery powered to allow pumping water to the home. He presumed two interior doors led to bedrooms. His gaze was particularly drawn to the black baby grand piano in a corner of the living area.

He remarked, "What a beautiful piano."

When the bowls with berries and shortcake were ready to be served, Amanda called to the boys, who were sitting on the porch steps. "Come and get some berries."

They came into the house only long enough for each to get a bowl and a spoon then returned to the porch to eat. The three adults sat at the dining table in the kitchen.

"I trust you had a useful talk," said Doctor Harvey.

"It is so wonderful to visit with another woman, especially Johanna who shares so much information," said Amanda. "Do you think Raymond's leg is healing well? He seems healthy to me. Is there anything more I should be doing?"

"He is doing very well," he replied. "I will examine his leg and the cast more closely before we leave today."

After eating the berries and then assessing Raymond's leg and cast, Doctor Harvey thanked Amanda and assured her the leg had healed nicely thus far. He said, "I think he will be ready to walk without crutches by the time school begins in September. You are doing a terrific job."

Johanna and Doctor Harvey each used the outhouse before departing. They thanked Amanda and the two boys for being splendid hosts. Then they drove away from the neat, clean house in the beautiful small valley and down the long, bumpy driveway to Reservation Creek Road.

"What is your estimate for when she will deliver?" he asked as they began the return trip north.

"Her last menstrual period was in mid-December, so I think the baby will come in September, maybe early October," she replied. "She has given birth twice before so she knows what is in store for her. We discussed finding a place in town to live as her due date approaches. She is strongly inclined to be in her own home. When Raymond was born, Axel was the only one with her at home during the delivery. She is a brave woman.

"However, beginning in September she wants to live in a place closer to Howard School so Axel would not need to ride a horse ten miles each day for sixth grade classes. Raymond would be able to attend first grade at Howard, too. If she does this she would be much closer to town when the baby comes. I am going to visit her again in August to learn more of her plans."

While he listened he pictured Marie at this stage of her pregnancy. She was so happy, so optimistic. They both were. He grew increasingly concerned about Amanda giving birth unattended—whether five or fifteen miles from town—without a telephone, electricity, or automobile.

"Look out!" yelled Johanna. The Hudson had drifted to the right edge of the road and the passenger side tires were only a few inches from the deep ditch paralleling the road.

He heard Johanna's warning and saw how close the automobile was to the ditch. He jerked the steering wheel to the left quickly, returning the tires to the ruts in the road. "Sorry," he said. "I was listening too carefully to your report. I'll concentrate on the road."

"What do you think of her plans for delivery and getting her boys closer to school?" asked Johanna.

"I am concerned," he said. "However, her options are limited. After you see her in August I'd like to talk with you to reassess her options."

After a minute he continued, "When we get to the River Valley

Road, I'd like to stop briefly to visit Herman Mueller and his niece, Gerde. Would you have time to do that before we return to town?"

"That would be fine," she replied. "I'll be going straight to Miles City from Forsyth. I have no other appointments scheduled today. I'll see Doctor Lindeberg tomorrow morning and then drive back to Colstrip Road to talk with the pregnant teenager and her parents."

"Good," he said. "I'd like for you to meet Gerde. She is eighteen and came here from Germany right before the war began. Her mother, Herman Mueller's sister, wanted to move her entire family here, perhaps sensing the tragic events that were coming. Now Gerde is here but her family has not been able to come. She is understandably depressed, having trouble eating and sleeping. I want to check on her and also see if she is someone you might add to your home visit list."

"I look forward to meeting her," said Johanna.

As they descended from the plateau toward the river valley, they saw the tree-lined river in the distance, smelled the grass hay fields, and felt a sense of wonder at the beauty of the setting. At the junction of Reservation Creek Road and River Valley Road, Doctor Harvey turned left away from town and drove a few miles to the Mueller ranch. Once at the house he and Johanna stepped out of the automobile and exchanged greetings with Herman Mueller and his wife, Jana.

Their two children were standing near the house, but Doctor Harvey did not see Gerde.

"Is Gerde here?" He asked. "I'd like to talk with her and have her meet Johanna, who is a public health nurse. I think Gerde may enjoy talking with Johanna."

"Ja, she is here," replied the rancher.

"I will get her," said his wife who was walking into the house. A moment later she returned with Gerde at her side.

"Hello, Gerde," said Doctor Harvey. "I'd like you to meet Johanna, who is a nurse. Perhaps the three of us could walk." He gestured toward the Yellowstone River only about 200 yards from where they stood. Between cottonwood trees lining the bank of the half-mile-wide river they could see it was nearly overflowing from spring snowmelt.

"Guten Tag," Gerde said to Johanna, who extended her hand as an additional greeting. "Have you seen this part of the river before?"

"No," replied Johanna, even though she was familiar with most of the river from Hysham to Miles City. "Please show us."

Doctor Harvey nodded to Herman, "We'll be back before long. We just want to have a short visit today."

Herman replied, "Gut. I will wait here." The children had dispersed and his wife made her way inside.

Gerde walked ahead to where the path cut between the last two cottonwood trees before reaching the riverbank. She turned and said, "See. Castle Butte."

She pointed across the river to a conspicuous rock formation jutting upward north of the river. "It reminds me of ein Schloss by the Rhine River near meine home."

Johanna stepped beside Gerde and said, "I have never been to the Rhine. It must be beautiful."

"Oh, es ist wunderbar," said Gerde. "I hope meine Mutter und meine Geschwister are well. I would like to see them now."

Johanna hugged Gerde and said, "You'll see them again, I know you will. I am sure they miss you very much."

Doctor Harvey asked Gerde how she was sleeping.

"I sleep a little more now. I take the medication jede Nacht," she responded.

"Are you eating more?" he asked.

"Nein. I do not eat very much. But I am not hungrig."

"I will leave another prescription," he said. "When you and your uncle go to town you can get more medication."

She nodded.

"I think it would be helpful if Johanna visited you now and then, too," he continued. "You could talk with her about many things."

He looked at Johanna hoping this plan was acceptable to her, and she nodded in affirmation.

Gerde looked at Johanna, back at Doctor Harvey, then at Johanna before saying, "It would be wunderbar to talk with you more."

Then she asked with more animation than he had seen from her before, "Could you come? When could you come?"

Johanna replied, "I would love to get to know you better. I could visit again tomorrow afternoon around one. Would that be a good time for you?"

"Ja, wunderbar," was Gerde's reply.

They walked back to the house, thanked Herman Mueller for the opportunity to visit, and confirmed the plan for Johanna to come again. Johanna hugged Gerde once more before Doctor Harvey started the Hudson. As they drove away, he and Johanna waved at Gerde and the Mueller family, who had gathered by the house to see them off.

On the trip back to Forsyth they shared observations about Gerde.

He said, "She is depressed. I am not sure the opium solution is helping her to sleep. I have a feeling though, that your visit and anticipation of another one is more therapeutic for her than all the medications at the pharmacy would be."

Johanna replied, "I'll be happy to visit her on days I am in this area, probably every second or third week. She is a lovely girl, very lonely. She needs a friend."

He reflected on this. By six o'clock that evening, he and Johanna arrived in Forsyth. He asked if she would like to have supper at the café before she drove to Miles City. She politely declined, saying she wanted to finish the drive before she had a meal and relaxed. He thanked her for the work she was doing.

CHAPTER EIGHT

July 1917

Doctor Harvey and Frances Olson ascended the steps of the neoclassical Rosebud County Courthouse. They had come to discuss school vaccination and quarantine policies with one of the county commissioners. The courthouse had a copper dome atop an octagonal tower and had opened in 1914 near Main Street at the east end of town. Despite the classical architecture everything about it seemed new. At the top of the stairs they looked upward at the colossal portico before opening the large wooden door to enter the second floor of the building.

Before going to the commissioners' offices on the second floor, they continued up a magnificent stairway to the third floor where the courtroom and judge's chambers were located. On the third floor they gazed up at the rotunda, which was circled by marble columns and topped by a wheel and spokes and colorful stained glass. Below the glass were four murals with Biblical scenes emphasizing obedience, reverence, justice, and defense of liberty. In the latter mural a sturdy female figure held a sword in her right hand and the U.S. flag across her left arm.

After viewing the third floor they descended again to the second. Some decorations from the Fourth of July were still posted even though the celebration had occurred nearly three weeks before. That year the celebration had been bigger and more boisterous than ever. A parade had begun at the west end of Main Street and progressed through town, with some participants carrying banners exuding patriotic fervor. There were also smaller signs displaying mistrust of Germans.

By the time all of the parade participants and many of the towns-people who had cheered the parade had reached the courthouse lawn, the assembled crowd consisted of more than 300 people. Speeches by elected officials were followed by the largest-yet fireworks display for Forsyth.

On the second floor were offices of the county registrar, the county clerk, and the county commissioners. When they entered the door to the commissioners' offices, a commissioner greeted them with a deep, authoritative voice.

"Welcome. Please have a seat," he said, motioning toward a large table surrounded by eight chairs. "I have been looking forward to talk-ing with you."

Frances Olson said, "Thank you for meeting with us. We'd like to discuss an issue important to the health of students in the county in preparation for convening school again in a few weeks."

"Well this will be an interesting change from the tax assessment, road, and bridge topics that have been dominating our meeting agen-das," replied the commissioner. "It looks like the damned river has fi-nally receded so the bridge work can get underway. What should we be doing for the health of students?"

"Doctor Harvey and I have reviewed our current vaccination and quarantine policies and have recommendations for your consideration," said Frances. "Perhaps Doctor Harvey could begin our presentation?"

"Of course, it is a pleasure to see you again, Doctor," said the com-missioner, now seated in a chair across the table from them.

"It is always a pleasure to talk with you, commissioner," replied Doctor Harvey. "As you know I am serving as the county health officer while Doctor Huene is with the Army Medical Corps."

"Yes, I understand he is at Fort Riley and likely to be away for some time while this war goes on," the commissioner responded. "I appreci-ate your willingness to serve in this role."

"I'll get right down to business in respect of your time," said Doctor Harvey. "First, I'll review the current policy and then recommend an addition to that policy."

The commissioner nodded and motioned toward a pitcher of water and glasses as if to ask if his guests would like something to drink.

Doctor Harvey continued, "The purpose of communicable disease rules is to prevent or limit the spread of communicable diseases. With respect to schools in the county, the current rules require isolation and exclusion from school of those students with certain communicable diseases, including whooping cough, poliomyelitis, and epidemic spinal meningitis. The rules do not now allow exclusion from school of any students who are not ill but who have been exposed to certain communicable diseases. This practice is called quarantine and has been used for centuries to control disease spread. For one communicable disease, smallpox, there is a vaccine to prevent the disease. The current rules encourage but do not require this vaccination for students to attend school.

"As you likely know, several cases of smallpox occurred in school-age children during the spring. The ill students were excluded from school and isolated at their homes. However, students who were not ill but had not been vaccinated were not automatically excluded, or quarantined, from school. While we do not know the exact number of unvaccinated students, we do know at least five unvaccinated students were exposed to ill students at school before the ill students were isolated. At least one of the smallpox cases this spring was an unvaccinated student who had been exposed to the disease at school.

"This brings me to the recommended addition to the current disease control rules. We recommend for control of smallpox that the rules should include two new sections: first, when an unvaccinated student is known to be exposed to a person with smallpox, the unvaccinated student must be excluded from school for fourteen days from the date of last exposure to a case of smallpox; and second, in order to attend school in Rosebud County a student must be vaccinated with smallpox vaccine."

He concluded by asking, "Do you have questions?"

"Well, yes, I do have questions about such a policy," the commissioner said forcefully.

Frances had warned Doctor Harvey this commissioner often railed against regulations and rules. He seldom missed an opportunity to criticize the federal income tax established—he would say perpetrated—in 1913. He had faced an election challenger who had argued the commissioner himself had become a perpetrator of rules and regulations.

Frances felt if this commissioner could be persuaded to support a new vaccination policy, other commissioners would probably agree also.

"Thank you for the clear presentation. However, if a new rule required the use of quarantine in the situation you described, why also require vaccination? Is it necessary to require vaccination when the authority to use quarantine exists?"

"Thank you for this important question," responded Doctor Harvey. "If I were to recommend to school officials to identify unvaccinated students who had had contact with smallpox, some practical issues could delay quarantine steps. First, school records of vaccination status are not now complete, so identifying unvaccinated students would become time consuming. Second, the absence of a vaccination scar does not always mean a child is unvaccinated, so it would be necessary to contact students' parents. Third and probably most challenging, when school officials advise a parent their child is not allowed to attend school unless vaccinated, some parents would object because vaccination is counter to their religious beliefs."

He looked at Frances and asked, "Would you like to say more?"

"We would have problems trying to follow the quarantine recommendation," she said. "Even when we explained the choice between getting vaccinated to stay in school or staying away from school for fourteen days if not vaccinated, some parents would object strongly to having their child denied school entry."

After a brief pause she continued, "Of course we would do our best to enforce the rule if there was one."

The commissioner looked skeptical. "If the rule were expanded as you are recommending, would the vaccination and quarantine requirements apply to teachers and other adults at school, too?"

Doctor Harvey answered, "That is a good question. The recommendation should be clarified to include quarantine for unvaccinated adult workers at schools and, perhaps, vaccination or well-documented history of having had smallpox should be a requirement for hiring a teacher or other school worker."

Turning to Frances he asked, "Would that be a problem for hiring?"

"No. I think that requirement could be instituted."

The commissioner asked, "Are there vaccines for other

communicable diseases, other than smallpox? And if so, should those vaccines also be required?"

Doctor Harvey replied, "Much effort has gone into trying to develop effective vaccines. However, at this time the only disease with potential to spread widely in schoolchildren for which a vaccine is available is smallpox."

The commissioner asked another question, "Can the government require vaccination of children to attend school? Is this legal?"

Frances replied, "Yes, Commissioner. Massachusetts established a smallpox vaccination requirement for school entry many years ago. One man's challenge to the vaccination requirement in that state went all the way to the U.S. Supreme Court. The court upheld the authority of a state to enforce compulsory vaccination laws."

The commissioner then asked, "What do we say to parents who object to having what they consider to be unnatural substances put into their children? And what about vaccines causing children to become sick?"

Doctor Harvey took a deep breath before beginning his response. "Smallpox has existed for centuries and caused enormous suffering and death. It is a part of the natural world and needs to be controlled. However, in rare instances a child given a vaccine can have a reaction and become ill. We need to weigh this risk against the protection the vaccine provides to almost all children. For the community, the schools, and the children, vaccination is very beneficial. It is the best way to prevent smallpox and protect children."

He could see the commissioner was far from convinced by this logic but he saw little chance that further elaboration would gain support at this time.

The commissioner said, "Thank you both. I will give this recommendation some thought and mention it to the other commissioners."

When Doctor Harvey and Frances stood to leave, the commissioner continued, "At least our registration and draft activities have been running smoothly. Our enlistment quota will be met, but the number of draftees will surely increase if the war goes on much longer."

The local draft board, established in May, consisted of this commissioner, the county sheriff, and a physician. A registration process to identify draft-eligible men ages twenty-one to thirty had been established. A questionnaire was being used to classify men into five categories ranging from Class 1, men with no claim to exemptions, to Class 4, men with a dependent wife and child, and Class 5, alien men, especially those who were German or Austrian. An examination by a physician was being used to assess physical qualifications. The first registration had identified men who would entrain into the military on September 3, 1917. More registration days would follow.

The registration process was occurring in counties statewide and was coordinated by the State Draft Board in Helena. It was time consuming with no compensation for draft board members. Doctor Harvey wondered if the activity could be sustained by patriotic feeling alone. Although he was not directly involved at this time, either as an age-eligible man or as a physician to conduct physical examinations, he knew he needed to remain aware of this activity.

The commissioner mentioned the Espionage Act passed by the U.S. Congress in June and said, "This law will help prevent support of our enemies during this war."

Doctor Harvey wondered exactly how a resident of Rosebud County could acquire or convey information with intent to interfere with the operation of U.S. military forces. He thought an action to obstruct recruiting or enlistment into the military seemed quite unlikely in a rural area like this but replied, "It will be important to remain vigilant."

The commissioner concluded, "If there are traitors here in Rosebud County, we will identify them. It's part of our duty to defend liberty, just like Lady Liberty in the picture outside the courtroom upstairs. Thank you for bringing the vaccination and quarantine issue to my attention."

After Doctor Harvey and Frances left the courthouse, she said she did not think the commissioner was likely to pursue a revised quarantine policy. She said, "I'm going home to have some supper."

The mention of supper reminded him he was hungry. He knew a trip to the café would overcome this problem. However, he was troubled by thoughts of other problems much less likely to be so readily resolved. He knew the current policy for controlling smallpox among students could be improved, although it did not seem likely this would

be achieved easily. He was also dismayed by the emphasis the commissioner placed on identifying traitors, the same emphasis he had heard
expressed by several townspeople in recent weeks. The intensity of the
feelings about the alleged danger posed by neighbors who happened to
be from Germany was especially troubling. He knew there was no vaccine to help control this.

CHAPTER NINE

October 1917

Autumn had arrived. Each day, sunup was later and sundown earlier. Temperatures during the day were cooler and during the evening below freezing. The color of leaves on the maple, chokecherry, and cotton-wood trees had changed from green to yellow. The wind brought biting cold air to dispatch the leaves from trees and rustle those already on the ground. Ranchers were busy trying to complete harvest activities. Townsfolk were wearing longer, warmer coats as they bustled about.

So many fallen, thought Doctor Harvey as he drove his Hudson on River Valley Road west of town during the late afternoon. He was looking at the multitude of fallen leaves under the cottonwood and box elder trees between the Yellowstone River bank and River Valley Road but thinking of reports from Europe of the hundreds of thousands of dead soldiers and civilians in what some were calling the Great War.

That morning at his office he had seen a woman who told him she felt too weak to care for herself. Yet she knew she had to care for her children and her ill, aging mother. The weakness, the lack of sleep, the loss of appetite, and the absence of energy she described were surely caused by her despondency, her utter grief. The grief had begun after she had opened the door of her home to see a soldier in dress uniform, ribbons neatly lined over his heart on his coat, and shoes perfectly pol-ished. His deep, caring voice said he regretted to inform her that her son had died during a training exercise. She knew he said more about a grateful nation, but she could not remember exactly what—nor could she remember how she became seated on the rocking chair in her living room. During the week since she received this news, she had eaten little, slept less, and showed no interest in her own cleanliness or maintenance of her home. Her sister had brought her to his office. According to the very concerned sister, the husband was as grief stricken as his wife.

Doctor Harvey wrote a prescription for tincture of opium. Taking this potion each evening might help the grieving mother sleep. He told the sister there was no medication to treat the underlying cause of the problem; only time and understanding of those close to her could begin to mend her badly broken heart. Still he had thought to himself that some patients would have intractable, pathologic grief and require institutional care. He knew this woman would not be the only grieving parent he would see during the coming weeks.

He found himself thinking more and more of the limitations of medicine, his inability to cure many of the maladies appearing in his office day after day. A young boy with diabetes was an example. He was always thirsty, always urinating, and his mother was doing her best to grapple with the recommended diet. This young boy would likely die before becoming an adult, and contemporary medicine had little to offer to alter that fate. A young adult man with Rocky Mountain spotted fever was another example. He had told of a fever and skin rash and recalled a tick bite to support the diagnosis, but whether he recovered or declined would be little affected by any treatment now available. Still another example was an older woman with joints so swollen and deformed she had trouble holding a cup of tea let alone helping care for her grandchildren, as she wanted most of all to do. So many illnesses he wanted to treat but for which no effective treatment was available.

These thoughts always culminated with an image of his wife entering the last trimester of pregnancy and so optimistic about being a parent. Then within a week her ankles swelled, her kidneys failed, her blood pressure soared, and she and the baby were gone. Why could he not have done more? This question, still unanswered, stuck in his mind.

However, there were diseases, notably injuries, for which his training had prepared him to provide effective treatment. This afternoon he was going to visit Amanda, who had delivered a baby girl in late August. She was now living with the baby and her two sons in a two-room dwelling at Finch Junction. Living there allowed both Axel and Raymond to attend Howard School where classes for grades one through high school were provided. He expected Raymond would have returned from school this late in the afternoon. He wanted to examine the young boy's right leg now six months after his fracture had been realigned and stabilized.

Finch Junction was about halfway between Forsyth and Hysham on the Northern Pacific Railroad line. The unincorporated town had been named for a Northern Pacific executive, a superintendent of dining cars. Like other section stops every seven to ten miles along the railroad line, it was home to a depot and a section crew. Since 1914 it was also home to a post office.

The one-story, wood-frame building in which Amanda and her children had lived since school began was near the depot. As he approached he saw Raymond and another young boy playing with a ball in front of the building. He parked his automobile and asked, "Hello, Raymond. Is your mother home?"

He replied, "Yes. She is inside. I'll tell her you're here."

Raymond entered the building and a moment later reappeared with his mother at his side. She was holding gently in her arms a small bundle wrapped in a pink blanket. She looked very tired despite her smile and ramrod straight posture.

"Welcome, Doctor," she said. "Won't you come in and have some tea?"

He stepped over the doorsill and entered a room with a sink, icebox, wood stove, table, three wooden chairs, a bed, and a crib. He saw another bed in a small adjoining room. From the ceiling hung an electric cord and a light bulb.

He looked at Amanda. "This must be your new baby," he said. "May I see her?"

"Yes. This is Helen. Would you like to hold her while I heat water for tea?" she replied.

He took the bundle and looked at the entirely innocent face of the sleeping baby. "She is beautiful," he said.

He asked, "How are you doing? It must not be easy to care for an infant and your two boys by yourself in temporary living space away from your homestead."

She did not reply at first while she prepared cups, saucers, spoons, and sugar to serve with the tea. Then she said, "As long as my boys are well and my baby healthy I will be fine. My husband, Charles, comes some days but he needs to be at the homestead most of the time to care for our animals, mend fences, and prepare the house and barn for winter. When he comes he brings milk and eggs. Yesterday he brought some squash, the last thing in our garden this year. On the next trip he will bring more wood for the stove."

He found her response informative but tangential to his question. "You have very fortunate children and a caring husband," he said. "How are you doing? You look tired as most mothers with an infant do. Do you have a friend, another woman, with whom to talk and share ideas?"

She replied with a firm, determined voice. "Doctor, you are very kind to be so concerned. I am fine. Helen is my third baby and I know I will be very tired for many months while I care for an infant. I moved here for Axel and Raymond to be closer to school. My children are blessings to me. There is nothing I would rather do than care for them."

She paused and continued, "I do talk with other women here. I see the woman next door nearly every day. On Thursdays some women from town bring bread and pies to sell to section crew workers. We visit when they come. And Johanna still visits me every other week. I am seeing other women more often here than I would on the homestead. I feel good about that!"

"I am happy to learn of your friendships. If there is anything with which I might help, please tell me," he said. "I would like to examine Raymond again while I am here. He appears to be getting along well."

"Of course, I will call him into the house," she replied.

The baby had begun crying. Amanda changed the diaper and was breastfeeding the now quiet infant while Doctor Harvey examined Raymond's leg. It had healed remarkably well. He looked at the wear patterns on the heels of Raymond's shoes. There was no evidence for a disparity in leg length between right and left. He questioned the boy and the mother about Raymond's activities. His strength and balance seemed unencumbered. The status of this busy, growing boy was good.

Before leaving he thanked her for the tea and told her Raymond's leg had healed and his leg bone was supporting an active, growing youngster.

During the drive back to town he reflected on his visit and about some egregious health problems persisting in the county. One physician had told him of a homesteader family found dead in their cabin in 1914. Three children ages three to seven and their mother were found by the father who had been working in Roundup for two weeks. The cause of death for the children was diphtheria—for the mother a self-inflicted gunshot. Even if these children had been brought to a physician, timely delivery of diphtheria antitoxin and round-the-clock monitoring of severely ill children would not have been easily accomplished in a town with no hospital.

A rancher had told him of another family demise that occurred in 1915. The rancher had been asked to take a team of horses and a wagon to town to get a casket and return the casket to a neighbor's homestead. By the time he delivered the casket it was 11:00 p.m., and by the time the body was buried, 1:30 a.m. The deceased was a child with whooping cough. A physician from town had also come to the homestead. The next day the rancher was asked to pick up and deliver another casket to the same homestead. Another child had died, also with whooping cough. The second casket had been too large for the grave dug for the child by neighbors. The rancher helped enlarge the grave so the body and casket could be buried. He had asked if there were any other ill children in the family; there were two. The next day he delivered another casket for another burial.

Doctor Harvey wondered if vaccines could be developed to prevent deaths from infectious diseases such as diphtheria and whooping cough. If accomplished this would certainly be a cause for celebration. He also thought about some marvels to be celebrated already. Electricity powered pumps for delivering water to homes and lights for illuminating the homes. Telephones made it possible to talk with people whether they were near or far away. Radio, whether electric or battery operated like the one at the Swensen home, made it possible for ranchers and homesteaders to hear the Metropolitan Opera as well as reports of fighting in Europe. And railroads and the U.S. Mail allowed persons in Rosebud County to purchase items from Chicago almost as readily as from Forsyth.

That morning at Doctor Harvey's office, May had asked if he had begun preparing for Christmas yet. She had. The topic seemed premature to him, but as she described some of her preparation he began to think maybe he, too, should be taking steps to be ready. She had a list of people to whom she wanted to give a gift—for some more than one gift. When she began listing the gifts, she had concluded that some were items not available at stores or shops in Forsyth. Some might be available in Billings or Miles City if she journeyed there. But that morning she was studying a Sears Roebuck catalog. When would she need to place orders to allow gift items to be delivered to Forsyth in time for her to wrap them? May's planning stimulated him to think about the coming holidays. He resolved to send greetings and gifts to his brother and to Marie's parents.

He was nearing Forsyth now, crossing the railroad tracks on the western edge of town. The railroad was essential for much of American life. Not only was mail transported by railroads but so were people, crops, and cattle. He realized, though, the role of railroads could change, as had the role played by steamboats and horse-drawn wagons once railroads arrived. Already townspeople and ranchers were using automobiles to travel to places they had previously visited by rail, and ranchers were beginning to move crops and cattle to market in trucks with internal combustion engines rather than railroad cars pulled by steam-powered engines. The presence of the railroad in Forsyth was the essential reason he was now practicing medicine here. He wondered if he would continue to practice in this rural setting.

When he arrived in town he parked his Hudson and walked to his room in the Annex of the Alexander Hotel. After a devastating fire had destroyed several buildings on the Choisser Block in June, new brick buildings, including a new three-story structure behind the Alexander Hotel, had been completed. Doctor Harvey had moved into a new apartment in the Annex. The apartment had electricity, telephone, running water, and a bathroom. He considered his living arrangement now to be thoroughly modern.

He was hungry and prepared a sandwich with bread May had given to him the day before and cheese from the icebox. He sliced an apple into quarter sections and sat at the table near his bed. He was more tired than he had anticipated after a drive to Finch Junction.

He joked with himself. Maybe he had been thinking too much, about too many things? Contemplating insoluble problems as well as the wonders of modern life unimaginable a generation or two ago was enough to tire anyone.

After using the bathroom he sat on his bed intending to read the latest issue of the *Journal of the American Medical Association.* However, it was Marie and not the medical articles dominating his thoughts. He recalled one of his mother's frequent sayings. "Sometimes it is harder than you think not to think of something," she would say.

He continued to look at the journal and to sip Flying U Rye from a glass.

CHAPTER TEN

January 1918

Doctor Harvey stepped from the sidewalk into the mercantile. Outside it was so cold his shadow had frozen to the sidewalk. He was wearing a flannel-lined, hip-length jacket, a warm cap with earflaps, and a worn pair of gloves. He had come to buy a warmer pair of gloves. Two weeks ago he had joined a group of townspeople in front of the courthouse at midnight to welcome the New Year. The temperature had been near zero and a strong wind had barreled in from the east.

He had asked a man standing next to him if the wind always blew this way. The man had replied, "No, sir. Sometimes it blows that-a-way," motioning with his thumb in the opposite direction. Doctor Harvey had not been able to feel his hands and vowed to get a new pair of gloves.

The store occupied one floor and contained a wide variety of merchandise including an array of winter clothes items. The goods were displayed on a line of waist-high tables down the middle of the room and in cabinets and shelves along the walls. The shelves covered the walls all the way up to the fifteen-foot ceilings. This made it necessary to use a ladder to reach the highest shelves.

Doctor Harvey walked to the back of the room toward the shelves covered with scarves, gloves, and earmuffs. He was glad these shelves could be reached without using a ladder. He slipped his hands into a pair of leather gloves. They were stylish and would keep his hands warm while he drove his Hudson. He also slipped on a pair of woolen mittens.

These were less stylish but much warmer than the leather gloves. He selected a gray woolen pair to purchase.

He saw the bank cashier looking at boots in a nearby section of the store and greeted, "Hello. Good day to be inside."

The banker nodded and replied, "I thought last January was cold but so far January 1918 has been one for the record books. It is mighty good to be inside today. I heard someone froze to death in town the other night."

"Yes," said Doctor Harvey. "The sheriff found a man's body near the railroad track east of town earlier this week."

He opted not to elaborate about the assumption that the man had frozen to death. A large gash on the left side of the man's head had been attributed to a fall onto the edge of a railroad tie. The fall had also been attributed to drunkenness because a near-empty bottle of whiskey had been found near the body. He had thought the death was as likely due to blunt force trauma as to hypothermia, but the non-physician county coroner had concluded a drunken man had frozen to death.

Doctor Harvey continued to wonder if this conclusion might have been biased by the identification determined during the cursory death investigation. The determination was based on a union membership card found in the man's coat pocket. The IWW card associated this man with the Industrial Workers of the World, presumed by Loyalty Leagues around the state to be seditious. Could this man's trauma have been intentional rather than accidental? Was the whiskey bottle his or might it have been left at the scene by someone else? The cause and manner of death had not seemed entirely established in Doctor Harvey's view.

"Well, I hope he wasn't draft age," said the banker. "We need to keep sending men to the military."

Doctor Harvey commented, "Since draft age will be expanding to eighteen to forty-five years, more men will be eligible. This man appeared to be in the expanded age group but there was no indication he was from Rosebud County."

"I understand we've had few volunteers since April and May," said the banker. "Now only drafted boys are joining."

Doctor Harvey would be thirty-five this year and was more cognizant of the draft now than he had been last year when draft age was twenty-one to thirty. While still in Illinois in 1916, he had considered joining the Army Medical Corps. But when the opportunity to come to Forsyth arose, he decided that maintaining the practice of a physician who had joined the Army Medical Corps would be his way to support the war effort. However, if a draft notice came to him now he would enlist and presumably be assigned to the Army Medical Corps himself.

The banker continued, "Sad news has been coming from the front, too. Some Canadian boys were killed in the battle at some place called Passchendaele. Many were wounded and are in hospitals in France. We need to show our support for the families with sons in uniform because those boys will be in battles soon. We certainly should not allow German sympathizers to move about in the community spreading doubts."

The tenor of his voice was rising and his lips were pursed. "Judge Crum should be dismissed from his position. He should be locked up. And some Kaiser-loving German ranchers should be sitting right beside him in the lockup."

Doctor Harvey was aware of talk of impeachment against Judge Crum, who lived in Forsyth and served as the district court judge. He had provided advice to a county resident of German background who had been accused of espionage. This led to allegations against Judge Crum. Doctor Harvey thought the judge had as many supporters as accusers among townspeople here. He recalled the conversation he had overheard between the banker and a rancher at the café in the spring. The concerns he had heard then about espionage or sabotage seemed less vehement, less hateful than what he was hearing now.

He replied, "If I understand correctly the governor has decided to convene a special session of the legislature next month to consider the concerns you have."

"Damn time, too," said the banker. "Those legislators have been sitting on their thumbs long enough. We need to be sure collaborators are dealt with and sympathizers are monitored closely. It's also time to know how many guns are in the hands of the Kaiser's followers right here in Montana."

Mercifully, Doctor Harvey felt, the banker's wife—who had been on the opposite side of the store—came to her husband's side. She said, "Hello Doctor. It is so nice to see you."

She locked her arm with her husband's as if ready for a stroll and said, "Come, dear. I must get back to the house."

The banker looked at her with approval and replied, "Of course, dearest. I have finished looking at clothes today."

To Doctor Harvey he said, "Nice talking with you. Those gloves will be very useful this winter."

After the couple departed, Doctor Harvey purchased the woolen gloves, talked with the store's owner, and left.

On the sidewalk he met both the county commissioner and Frances Olson, who said, "Good day, Doctor Harvey. The commissioner and I were just talking about the vaccination and quarantine items. The Board of Commissioners will not be acting on these. If you have a few minutes let me buy coffee for the three of us at the café."

"A cup of coffee sounds life saving today," he responded.

At the café Alice asked if they wanted a table by the window, but Frances asked, "Could we have the table closest to the stove? That would help thaw us."

"Right this way," said the smiling waitress. "Would you like coffee, or maybe tea?"

"Just coffee today. Coffee all around," said Frances.

When Alice returned with piping hot coffee she said to the commissioner, "I hope you will be running for office again this year."

"Thank you," replied the commissioner, who would be seeking his third term if he ran again in November.

After Alice walked away he continued, "I was at a meeting in Bozeman recently and talked with one of the Gallatin County commissioners there. They had considered a policy to require smallpox vaccination for school entry and kicked up quite a storm. Some anti-vaccination folks had recruited a candidate to run for his position and damned near sent him packin'. They call themselves the Freedom League. The other Gallatin County commissioners didn't want to fight those folks and I don't think Rosebud County commissioners hanker to tangle with the Freedom League either. That's the tall and the short of why I doubt we will be taking any action on a vaccination requirement. We have plenty to do trying to help farmers get grain seed to grow wheat to feed the troops."

"I certainly appreciate your efforts. I am beginning to recognize how difficult it can be to establish policies," responded Doctor Harvey. "I continue to recommend a vaccination requirement for school entry, but it looks like quarantine will remain the only arrow in our quiver for smallpox control again this year."

Frances opined, "We encourage parents to have their children vaccinated and most do. But some simply will not consent to it."

Doctor Harvey replied, "Since the holidays are over and children have returned to school, we may need to use quarantine measures. I saw a three-year-old with measles last week. This child is isolated at home and I instructed the parents to keep their other children away from school for two weeks until we see if they come down with measles, too. However, with measles in the community I anticipate more cases. School-age children are likely to be exposed. We need to be prepared for quarantine steps."

Several thoughts had gone through his mind as he spoke. He had not been feeling optimistic. Was his medical practice making a difference? Was medical science just too limited to help women to survive pregnancy, newborns to grow to be children, children to become adults, and adults to live long healthy lives? Shouldn't there be more than fresh air to offer a patient with tuberculosis?

Vaccination was a near miraculous way to protect people from disease, but why were so few vaccines available? Even when an effective vaccine was available to protect people from smallpox, how could he convince some parents and policymakers to at least protect children? If he continued to advocate for building a hospital, would the commissioners take action? Was his practice of patching wounds, mending fractures, prescribing to relieve pain or encourage sleep the best he could do for his patients?

Despite these doubts he looked at the commissioner and said, "For treatment of some illnesses, a hospital with skilled nursing care would be very useful. Might the commissioners support the building of a hospital here?"

"Maybe," was the commissioner's brief, noncommittal reply. "I hope you two will use the current quarantine policy to protect the schoolkids the best you can."

Alice returned to offer more coffee but all three declined. Frances gave her a dollar and said, "Thank you."

Doctor Harvey walked quickly to his room at the Annex. Once there he sat near the steam heat register and adjusted the supply valve to get more heat. As the room warmed he recalled what Johanna had told him the day before when she came to his office to share information from her home visits.

She had opened the conversation with a reminder, "You probably remember the unmarried, pregnant sixteen-year-old we discussed during our drive to the Swensen homestead last June. I was able to get the parents to talk with Doctor Lindeberg."

"Yes. I do remember. What has happened with that case?"

"The parents were reluctant to take their daughter to Miles City. The young girl and the parents did not feel the pregnancy could be ended. The parents, at least, said their religious beliefs prohibited that," she replied. "However, the parents and the girl agreed with a recommendation from Doctor Lindeberg for the girl to go to Helena to live at the Florence Crittenton Home and have the baby there."

He had heard about the home in Helena. Years ago a New Yorker named Crittenton had lost his daughter, Florence, to scarlet fever. He was despondent but had a religious awakening. He was determined to help what he called fallen women and wayward girls. He had founded nearly fifty shelters for single mothers, especially unwed expectant mothers, across the country. One of those shelters had operated in Helena for twenty years.

Johanna continued, "Well, in December she delivered a baby boy. I talked by phone with the matron. Arrangements had been made for the baby to be adopted. The girl saw the newborn only once after birth. She did not return to live with her family. Instead she is working as a housemaid for a well-to-do family in Helena. The matron told me the girl realized she would not be able to establish her own independence and care for an infant at the same time. The story is not entirely resolved, may never be. The girl has not disclosed to me, to Doctor Lindeberg, or to the matron who the father is."

He said, "Remarkable. How fortunate for her you were so helpful. How did you first learn of the pregnancy?"

"The circumstance was curious," Johanna replied. "I received a telephone call from the girl's mother. In retrospect I do not know from where she made the call. There was no telephone at their ranch. She asked if I could visit her daughter who, she said, had been acting strange and had been vomiting in the morning for several days. The mother said, 'I hope she is not pregnant.' She said this with a distaste I interpreted at the time to be parental disappointment. Now I wonder if the mother might have known pregnancy was likely and also known the man responsible for it. But she did not disclose any more information than necessary to get help for her daughter. The matron told me the girl showed no interest to contact her parents as the delivery date approached and has no contact with them now."

"Remarkable," he repeated.

Johanna then changed the topic to share additional information about another issue.

"I just came from the Mueller's ranch. Gerde communicates more easily now than when I began visiting her. You remember she spoke little, didn't move her arms or hands when she did speak, and her face was expressionless. She was eating little and had trouble sleeping. She was very lonely.

"She is still lonely, and misses her mother and siblings a great deal," Johanna continued. "However, she realizes separation from her family cannot be ended now. She is keeping a diary to give to her mother when the war is over. In the diary she records her activities and her feelings in German. She would talk with her mother about these things now if she could. Instead her goal is to share these thoughts with her mother when she sees her again. She is very motivated."

He observed, "She has created her own therapy, with your help of course!"

Johanna looked more concerned as she continued, "But now another issue has become very troubling for her. The Mueller family has become much more isolated as the war has gone on. Neighbors they considered to be friends have not visited for months, people they see during visits to town do not talk with them or exchange even brief greetings, and Herman Mueller is reluctant to take Gerde with him when he comes to town.

Gerde has overheard him and his wife talking about hateful comments some townspeople have made about Germans, and in some instances about the Mueller family in particular. Mr. Mueller does not want Gerde to be exposed to the hatefulness."

He shook his head and said, "This is terrible. I know some townspeople are projecting their fears about the war onto neighbors who happen to be German, but I like to think hatefulness is uncommon."

He had also wondered, although he had not mentioned this to Johanna, if some of the apparent xenophobia, a term he had learned in medical school, might be motivated by something other than war fears.

She added, "Gerde has become anxious, even fearful, about these anti-German feelings. She told me her uncle found a message nailed to a gatepost at the head of his driveway. The message said, 'Go back to Germany, Kaiser lover.' He has also found some fence around his land damaged in a way he thinks was purposeful."

He asked, "Do you know if he has reported this to the sheriff?"

She replied, "I don't know for sure but I think it is unlikely he would make a report."

He said, "I will look into this further. I appreciate learning the information you have shared."

He intended to talk with Herman Mueller about this. If he could avoid betraying confidentiality, he would also ask Sheriff Starr or a county commissioner about complaints like this. Some situations worthy of law enforcement attention would not be investigated unless complaints were filed. He suspected Herman had reported no more about his harassment than had the teenage girl in Helena about her likely molestation.

His room was now comfortably warm. That afternoon when he departed to his office, he did not readjust the steam heat supply valve so he could return to the same comfortable warmth that evening.

CHAPTER ELEVEN

June 1918

When Doctor Harvey left his office for lunch he noticed three young boys, probably ten or eleven years of age, on the sidewalk. They were walking quickly and turned right, out of sight onto Ninth Avenue. He imagined they were on their way to retrieve fishing poles before spending the afternoon in a shady spot near the Yellowstone River. The river was swollen by late spring snowmelt and unusually heavy rains, and many of the usual fishing spots were not safely accessible. Seeing the boys in early afternoon reminded him school was out for the summer.

During the spring he and school officials had conferred several times regarding quarantine steps after he had diagnosed measles in a schoolchild. He was relieved knowing large groups of schoolchildren would no longer be congregating at school daily for the next three months. If a case of measles occurred in a school-age child, school would no longer be a place for other children to be exposed.

On his way to the café he met the legislator Arthur Elliott, who said, "Good day, Doctor."

Arthur was wearing Levi Strauss denims, a long-sleeved cotton shirt, and well-worn boots. This attire was less formal than usual for a politician whose appearance was as much a hallmark as his bravado.

Doctor Harvey replied, "Good day to you. It must be nice to be home after all the activity in Helena this year."

Arthur boomed a reply as if launching a stump speech, "Indeed it is wonderful to be home. This is the best place on earth, especially after dealing with the turmoil at the legislature."

He paused momentarily as if to arrange his thoughts before proceeding. "A special session it was. We needed to take action before seditious sabotage spread any further."

Doctor Harvey admired the use of alliteration, but he knew he would be less impressed by the logic in what came next.

The legislator continued, "If that damned Bourquin had protected America and not supported the likes of a disloyal rancher, and if our damnable neighbor Crum was not collaborating with the Hun-helpers around here, we wouldn't have needed a special legislative session. But by God we have now made it clear Montanans can identify traitors and we need to put them away at Deer Lodge if need be."

The soliloquy was reaching a crescendo, "And as you know, we required counties to have guns registered, too. If push came to shove with the traitors and sympathizers, county sheriffs would at least know where the weaponry is."

While he listened to Arthur expound, Doctor Harvey recalled events about which he had read differing versions in the town's two newspapers and heard more than one point of view from folks around town. George Bourquin, the judge of the Butte District Court, was being widely criticized by groups feeling there should be more prosecutions of those accused of being traitors. Chief among these groups was the Montana Council of Defense. It had been established when President Wilson asked each state to create a council to help with the war effort. The Council in Montana, with enthusiastic support of county councils of defense, including one in Rosebud County, had focused on identifying and accusing alleged traitors.

One of the accused was a rancher, Ves Hall, from southern Rosebud County. He had strongly criticized American involvement in the war. The Rosebud county attorney had been designated to argue the case against Mr. Hall. The trial was first scheduled for Billings but subsequently moved to Helena. Judge Bourquin heard the Hall case and determined no law had been broken no matter how provocative the statements made by the German rancher. Judge Crum from Forsyth had testified on behalf of Mr. Hall.

The Montana Council of Defense and its supporters were livid about the Hall decision. They pushed for a special session of the legislature. The session had been held in February. At that session the legislature had impeached Judge Crum despite the fact he had resigned prior to the legislative hearing. Doctor Harvey had felt the impeachment proceeding was probably not necessary but it was certainly unfortunate because at the time Crum was trying to help care for his son who had cancer. The legislators had also enacted a Montana sedition law and a gun registration law during the special session.

The Montana law had been a model for the recently passed federal Sedition Act of 1918. In Montana use of the German language had been banned, German textbooks had been burned in Lewistown, and one pastor had had to seek an exception to the ban in order to preach to his church members who spoke only German. Arthur Elliott and his like-minded colleagues had been very busy thus far in 1918.

He asked the legislator, "How strong was the evidence that Ves Hall is a danger to our country? Judge Bourquin seemed to conclude there was no clear danger nor evidence for espionage, at least in the account I read in *The Democrat*."

Arthur stood even more erect than his usual perpendicular posture and fired back, "Jesus, Doctor! Have you been reading that apologist rag of a newspaper? At least a half dozen people heard Hall disparage our country's war preparation, and he said he wouldn't register for a draft. There was eyewitness testimony at the trial. Bourquin ignored the evidence, turned the bastard loose. So we tightened the law at the special session, made it harder for judges like Bourquin to stand in the way of justice."

Doctor Harvey decided to ask another question, even though he anticipated a similarly vitriolic reply. "Was an impeachment hearing for Judge Crum really necessary? I understand he resigned his position before the hearing began."

Arthur took a deep breath and appeared as puffed up as a sage grouse rooster before saying, "Damn if you haven't been spending too much time reading that rag. Of course we had to impeach Crum, set an example for other judges who might consider supporting traitors. Should do the same for Bourquin, but Wheeler keeps standing in the way. We need to get that wobbly-lover un-appointed, too. And, Doctor, let me offer you some friendly advice. You might want to pay more attention to the coverage in the *Times-Journal* and not rely on the slanted views published in *The Democrat.* Then the line of questioning you pursue might not be mistaken as sympathetic to the sedition occurring in our country."

Doctor Harvey demurred and replied only after a long pause. He wondered if Elliott realized the Levi denims he was wearing were designed by an immigrant from Bavaria. Doctor Harvey had read of threats to launch more judicial proceedings and of venomous criticism of Burton Wheeler, the federal district attorney in Montana.

He said, "Good to see you today."

"Good to see you as well, Doctor," replied the legislator, glancing at his pocket watch. "Please excuse me. I'm due at a meeting at the Masonic Temple."

They nodded at each other as Arthur Elliott began walking east toward the Masonic building and Doctor Harvey west to the café. He thought the parting much less friendly than the greeting had been. His concern about the intensity of hateful accusations levied against some county residents was further heightened.

At the café a cheerful and ever optimistic Alice greeted him. He felt this to be a therapeutic bonus to accompany whatever he ordered for a meal. As he sat in the spoke-backed wooden chair at a table by the window, Herman Mueller stepped into the café.

The German rancher asked the waitress, "Have you a place I can sit to have lunch?"

"Of course, Mr. Mueller, you are always welcome here," she replied. "Are you by yourself today?"

"Ya. I am by myself," he answered.

Doctor Harvey stood again and said, "Perhaps you would join me at this table. I am about to order a sandwich. I would enjoy talking with you if you would join me."

Herman replied, "I also would like to talk. Danke, thank you for offering."

When the two men were seated the waitress asked, "Would you like coffee, or maybe lemonade on a day like this?"

The rancher asked for coffee, no cream, no sugar, and Doctor Harvey requested lemonade, which sounded very appealing to him.

The waitress asked, "Do you know already what you would like to order?"

Doctor Harvey responded, "I would like a hamburger, please. As usual, not too well done."

Alice looked at him and said, "I will place the order and I know you will enjoy the sandwich. Let me mention something so if you hear the chef call me when the sandwich is ready you will know I placed the right order. The sandwich is now being called a ground-beef sandwich rather than a hamburger. Our owner received a notice from the local Loyalty League discouraging use of German language or words with German connotations. The letter included examples, and 'hamburger' was on the list; so was 'sauerkraut'. The League suggested naming these items Liberty Steak and Liberty Cabbage. At first our owner dismissed the notice, but he decided to comply with some suggestions as he heard more and more stories of Loyalty Leagues around the state bringing sedition charges against people judged to be transgressors. In the end he thought ground-beef sandwich was a sufficient name change."

She paused briefly, looked at Herman and continued, "I am sorry this is happening. I assure you, though, you are welcome here and we appreciate your business."

Doctor Harvey was disgusted by the logic apparently used to change the name of a sandwich. He said, "Thank you for telling me this. Since hamburgers are not available at this time I would like to change my order. May I have a ham sandwich with a slice of cheese in the sandwich, too?"

Herman said, "I also would like a ham sandwich with a slice of cheese."

Alice replied, "Of course gentlemen. I will take the orders to the kitchen now. Would either of you like to have a bowl of potato soup to go with your sandwich? The soup was prepared this morning and it is delicious."

Both men shook their heads to decline. Alice walked to the kitchen and a few minutes later returned with coffee and lemonade.

Doctor Harvey had begun a discussion with the rancher by simply asking how he and his family were doing. At first the reply had been very general; "getting by," "doing well," the rancher had replied. However, Doctor Harvey found these responses unconvincing.

He asked, "Have you or your family been troubled by the unfortunate activities such as Loyalty League investigations underway in this county since the Montana Sedition Law was passed by the state legislature?"

Herman began describing some events. Doctor Harvey perceived relief, understandable relief, within the burdened man as the discussion continued.

Herman mentioned, "Gerde is doing much better since you and the nurse visited. She especially enjoys the days the nurse comes to talk with her. I am grateful for what you have done. But there is still trouble. She worries for us."

Doctor Harvey queried, "Worries for you?"

Herman continued, "Ja. Our neighbor does not visit us now and does not invite us to dinner on Sunday any longer. When we visit town we hear when people call us krauts and Kaiser followers. Some merchants do not welcome us like they did before this war. At church a deacon took me aside and told me to stop singing hymns auf Deutsch. Meine Frau liebt the way the hymns sound auf Deutsch. Now we sing them auf Deutsch at home but not in church. Und meine fence has been damaged on purpose—I am sure not by accident. This allows my cattle to leave my pastures and move to my neighbors' pastures. I do not want my cattle to cause trouble so I ride my fenceline each morning to mend damaged spots. Gerde weiss diese things. She cares for us."

Doctor Harvey asked, "Have you reported the fence damage to the sheriff?"

Herman looked even more concerned than he had before. He replied, "I did tell the deputy sheriff but he asked how I could be sure the damage was not caused by my cattle? Cattle do not cut wires, do not break fence posts this way. I did not want to talk with him further. He was only interested in whether I had reported all my guns to the sheriff. I told him the only guns I had were two rifles and I had reported these to the sheriff in April when I learned of the registration requirement. I do not think the deputy sheriff believed me. He told me not to forget the June deadline to register all guns. He said he would be enforcing the law and violators, 'liars' he said, would be prosecuted. I have not talked any more with him or the sheriff."

Doctor Harvey felt a mix of anger and sadness about the events unfolding this year. He said, "I can sure understand why you would not want to talk further with either of them. I feel bad knowing what you and your family are going through. I hope this war ends soon and everyone in this community returns to caring for and supporting their neighbors."

The rancher replied with a skeptical tone, "Ich auch, I too, hope the war ends soon. Gerde is also very worried about her mother and siblings."

The waitress came with the ham sandwiches and asked, "Any more coffee or lemonade?"

Both men indicated yes and began eating their sandwiches.

While they ate the men talked about crop growth and weather, but Doctor Harvey kept thinking about the way some had turned against their neighbors. This left a sour taste in his mouth, much more sour than the lemonade he was drinking. He was afraid these events were likely to be amplified as the war went on, especially when reports of U.S. casualties came to Rosebud County. The American Expeditionary Forces were on the front line now. Casualties and severe injuries were certain to occur.

He wondered if these toxic feelings and actions were happening elsewhere or if Montana was the only place sedition fever was spreading. He knew, though, this epidemic of hatefulness and hurt must be spreading like an infection throughout the country. He had read of a German man named Prager who had been hung by a mob in East St. Louis. A government official there seemed to have justified the lynching by observing the residents had done so because they had felt the government would not punish disloyalty. Was Montana more affected than elsewhere? Did Rosebud County have the most virulent form of this malady? These thoughts disturbed him.

After the men finished the sandwiches they thanked the waitress for her excellent service. Doctor Harvey paid for both despite Herman's objection. He prevailed in the brief discussion of how the bill would be paid by suggesting they meet for lunch again and Herman would pay for both meals then.

As they stood and prepared to leave, the deputy sheriff walked by the window and looked into the café. Doctor Harvey perceived a menacing look but realized his own perception might be biased, influenced by the disturbing things he had heard from the rancher. Would he, himself, become more involved with the affliction turning neighbor against neighbor?

They left the café. Herman went to his Ford parked less than a block away. Doctor Harvey returned to his office for another busy afternoon seeing patients with a variety of diseases and discomforts. When he saw these patients he wondered how the community's affliction was affecting them—and if some might be perpetuating the spread of this affliction.

CHAPTER TWELVE

September 1918

Doctor Harvey was sitting in his straight-backed, wooden chair at the table in his third-floor room at the Alexander Hotel Annex. The coffee he was drinking tasted fine despite the fact he had simply reheated the pot he made the day before. Through the window he was looking northwest at a landscape not clearly visible to him a few minutes before, but once the sun had begun rising he could see rows of one- and two-story houses lining streets north toward the Yellowstone River. The homes and the downtown business district had been flooded in June when the river overflowed its banks. The deluge caused much damage, but the owners of businesses and homes had largely recovered now.

The cottonwood and the box elder trees near the river's edge were visible, leaves still green but after several chilly September nights about to don the orange and yellow colors they would display before dropping to the ground in a few more weeks, leaving tree skeletons to face the long autumn and winter.

The first patient appointment at his office was still two hours away. He sipped the coffee and previewed the day ahead. Schools had been back in session for three weeks and no unusual illness patterns had occurred. Still, he was cautious because of reports he had read of influenza among troops on the European war front and in several cities in the United States. He felt little sense of urgency, just caution. He anticipated seeing patients with tuberculosis, often called consumption, and heart failure, often called dropsy, but knew the usual unusual events might cause patients to visit his office. The snakebite season was winding down, but being kicked by a horse or bitten by a spider could prompt a visit to a doctor. Such events could lead to modifications of a schedule that seemed tidy at the beginning of the day.

He was grateful to have May working with him. Her ability to keep office activities running and to help patients and their families accommodate to changes was invaluable. He reminded himself to tell her more often how much he appreciated her work.

One event for the day was causing him considerable concern. That afternoon he would meet with officials of the local draft board and register to determine his eligibility status. This draft board had operated since May 1917 when the U.S. Congress enacted the draft. Three draft registration days had occurred for men ages twenty-one to thirty: June 5, 1917; June 5, 1918; August 24, 1918. Now a registration date for men ages eighteen to forty-five had been set. He was thirty-five and would register. He was aware of the criteria for most exemptions and deferrals but since he was healthy, not married, and had no dependents, he knew these exemptions would not apply for him. The criteria for an additional exemption category were not entirely clear to him. This category exempted men employed in agriculture, industry, or other occupations deemed essential to the war effort. He wondered if his local medical practice and health officer role would be deemed as one of the essential occupations.

Doctor Harvey thought he might be exempted because he was supporting the practice of another physician who had joined the Army Medical Corps. On the other hand there were other physicians in Forsyth. He had been thinking about whether or not to relocate when the war was over; perhaps he could get specialty training or practice in a city. Military medical officers were receiving $2,000 to $2,400 per year, which when augmented by allowances for quarters, fuel, and light was not substantially different from the income he had been generating here. If he were drafted he would comply. He had also considered joining the Volunteer Medical Service Corps and to be readily available to serve.

Enough forecasting of coming events, he thought. He finished his coffee, tidied his room, and went to his office. May was waiting when he arrived. She mentioned the patients with morning appointments and reminded him of a meeting with the draft board that afternoon. She also mentioned Sheriff Starr had called to request a meeting between noon and 1:00 P.M.

Doctor Harvey said, "Of course I will meet with the sheriff."

May replied, "I thought you would so I told him noon would be a good time."

He looked at her and said, "I hope you know how much I appreciate the work you do—the way you organize what would otherwise be quite chaotic."

She smiled and replied, "I know but I do like to hear you say so, too."

Among the patients he saw during the morning was a man with a painful, purulent abscess near the end of his right index finger. Doctor Harvey lanced the felon and instructed the man how to keep the skin in that area clean during the days the wound would be healing. Another patient was a young boy with fever and a blotchy red rash on his face. Doctor Harvey made a diagnosis and explained to the boy's mother the features of scarlet fever and the importance of isolating the boy from other children during the illness.

At noon he was writing notes in patient records when May knocked on the door of the examination room. He said, "Come in."

"Sheriff Starr is here now," she said.

He stood and said, "Please ask him to come right in."

A moment later Harold Starr was standing at the door.

"It is good to see you," Doctor Harvey said as he gestured toward a chair beside his desk. "Please come in and have a seat. Would you like some coffee or a glass of water?"

He strode into the room, his white, broad-brimmed cowboy hat in his left hand, and extended his right to shake hands with Doctor Harvey. He said, "Good to see you, too, Doctor. No thanks to the coffee. Your very efficient assistant offered the same when I arrived. I'm tempted to offer her a job. We could use such a pleasant and organized office manager. But I wouldn't feel right visiting your office and recruiting your assistant!"

Doctor Harvey replied, "I appreciate your reticence to recruit here. I would be quite lost if she were to leave! What brings you for a visit today? Last time we talked you had questions about a body your deputy found. I hope there is no need to assess a cause of death for another unfortunate soul."

Harold Starr, now seated by the desk, replied, "No. No unexplained deaths for study this time."

His facial expression turned more serious as he continued, "I'm afraid my visit today has a very different purpose. I'm hoping it is not really necessary, but there is something I need to mention to you."

Doctor Harvey was even more curious now than he had been before about this visit. "Well by all means let me know. Maybe there is a way I can be helpful."

"I will get right to the point," said Harold, looking intently into Doctor Harvey's eyes. "My deputy has told me you have been meeting with Herman Mueller and seem to be very friendly with him. I want to be sure you know he is being investigated by the Loyalty League and there is a chance he will be brought to trial on charges of sedition. I wouldn't want to see you drawn into the investigation or the charges."

Doctor Harvey was stunned. He was aware some townspeople had made accusations against people with German names for statements said to be seditious. He, himself, considered the statements cited to be far from intentional sedition. He had not seriously considered the possibility these accusations could become a basis for formal charges and trials. However, after hearing the sheriff's admonition he now wondered how rampant the sedition discussions were. Was this an epidemic? How could the spread of hypercritical or outright malicious thoughts and accusations be mitigated? If the etiology were bacterial, quarantine or lancing an abscess might help. But it was not bacteria causing disease. He was disturbed by the possibility that isolation or quarantine would be applied to persons accused rather than the persons spreading the epidemic.

He would not apologize for meeting with Herman Mueller or anyone else who happened to speak German or have relatives in Germany. Yet he was interested to learn more about the process of bringing someone to trial for alleged sedition.

He said, "I am entirely surprised to hear your concern. I am not aware of activities one would consider inciting rebellion against the government involving Mr. Mueller. Someone must be very concerned about this to consider having a trial."

Sheriff Starr looked very stern as he said, "I assure you, doctor, the situation is quite serious for more than one German sympathizer in this county. You recall the Ves Hall case and the hullabaloo it caused? Some folks feel his activity is just the tip of an iceberg and the whole iceberg needs to be exposed. Some trials are already scheduled for later this month, although Mr. Mueller has not been formally charged, yet. I just wouldn't want to see you drawn into this."

Several questions were circling in his thoughts. If questioning participation in the war was enough cause to go to a trial, then how many trials would need to be held for Montana residents who had posed the question? Was this a sufficient cause only for residents with German names? If not buying war bonds impeded the conduct of war, did inefficient movement of food and materials to support the war effort also qualify as a sedition offense? Since the federal government had judged it necessary to nationalize the railroads in July in order to ensure efficient delivery of food and goods, should railroad executives go on trial for their apparent failure to do this?

He realized there was little to gain from posing questions such as these to Harold Starr, so he simply asked about an account he had read in *The Forsyth Democrat.* "Did your deputy punch the attorney Canning at the Placer Hotel in Helena after Canning defended Mr. Hall before Judge Bourquin? Did that result in any disciplinary action?"

Harold Starr's face reddened. "My deputy sure as hell did punch that sympathizer. If any disciplinary action is in order it should be disbarment of the attorney for supporting disloyalty!"

He stood, walked toward the door, and continued, "I do need to get back to my office. I appreciate the opportunity to talk with you today. I hope you will give this some thought."

On his way out he placed his hat on his head and tipped the brim as a gesture of thanks to May.

After Harold Starr left, May looked at Doctor Harvey quizzically and said, "I hope that meeting went better than I suspect it did."

"It was important to have a discussion," was his brief reply.

He did not feel like having lunch so he went back into the examination room to review what he had heard and consider what steps he might wish to take.

The afternoon seemed to go quickly. He made a special effort to concentrate on diagnosis and treatment decisions for each patient so his concerns about sedition issues would not interfere.

After the last patient left he walked to the courthouse. From the lobby he went to the county clerk's office and requested a registration form.

A draft board member was there and seemed surprised to learn of the doctor's eligibility. "In my view your work is essential to the war effort, so we should proceed straight to an exemption with your registration."

However, another board member also standing there scratched his head and slowly added, "I think we'll need to review the guidance we received from the Selective Service System to confirm the criteria for that exemption before we make a determination."

Doctor Harvey responded, "I would expect you to do nothing less."

He and the board members exchanged ideas about the war, which was taking more and more lives; the weather, which was cold; and wildlife, which was abundant for hunting. Then he walked back downtown to his room at the Alexander Hotel Annex.

He poured a larger than usual glass of Flying U and sipped the oak-flavored whiskey while he reviewed the events of the day. Maybe enlisting in the Army Medical Corps would be a reasonable step to take. Maybe the sedition accusations would increase, or maybe dissipate when accusers thought more clearly about the events.

By the time he poured a third glass of Flying U, he was thinking of his wife, his stillborn child, his inability to help the ones who meant most to him. When he awoke the next morning, his head ached and he found the whiskey bottle on his table empty.

At his office that morning he placed a telephone call to Herman Mueller. He heard "Hello" at the other end of the line and asked, "Is this Herman?"

"Ja. Es ist me," came the reply.

"This is Doctor Harvey. Do you have time to talk for a few minutes?"

"Ja."

Doctor Harvey continued, "I am calling to tell you some things I have heard and to see if there is anything I can do to help."

He paused while silence persisted on the telephone line and then went on, "Yesterday Sheriff Starr told me the local Loyalty League has been investigating you. Are you aware of this?"

Again silence, but finally Herman responded, "Ja. Two members of that group came to my ranch last week. They questioned me at the front door of mein Haus! They asked if I bought war bonds, why we had not come to church since we were asked, told really, to stop singing hymns auf Deutsch, and if I am loyal to the Kaiser."

Doctor Harvey asked, "Did you answer their questions?"

"I did not feel I needed to answer. Why should I be questioned in this way, in mein eigenes Haus?"

Doctor Harvey replied, "And you do not need to answer me either. I am just wondering if there is something I can do to help."

Herman replied again, "Ja. I did not feel I needed to answer, but I did. I am concerned about what might happen to my family if this committee pursues me. I have heard about other German ranchers and business owners being accused of disloyalty and being threatened with trials, even with prison."

After another long pause he continued, "I told them I could not buy war bonds until I have paid a loan debt. I told them my family loves to sing hymns and worship God auf Deutsch but we were staying home to sing so we would not trouble anyone at church."

Doctor Harvey observed, "Once the League gets truthful answers like these maybe that will be the end of it? That should be the end of it!"

Herman said, "But there was one thing I would not do, and I doubt the League is done with me."

"What is it you would not do?"

He said nothing for a few moments but then replied, "They had a flag, a U.S. flag. Right there, standing in my own front door, I was told to salute. I could not do that. I told them I supported the United States and I was loyal to this country, but I did not think it was right to be told to salute a flag while I was in meinem eigenen Haus. I asked them if they were going to all homes in Rosebud County to tell everyone to stand in ihrem eigenen Haus and salute the flag? They did not answer. They said I would be hearing more from them."

Doctor Harvey was shocked to hear what had happened and to think about what else might be happening in the county, in the state.

He said, "I am sorry you have been treated this way. It is entirely uncalled for, entirely inappropriate."

Herman interrupted and said, "Do not forget, Doctor, my telephone line is a party line. I cannot be sure if someone is listening to our conversation. You may not want to share all your thoughts in this way."

Doctor Harvey was further shocked. Had the Loyalty League activities caused a longtime resident of Rosebud County, a citizen of the United States, to experience this type of intrusiveness, to consider whether or not he was under surveillance, to perceive a real threat to his own liberty?

He said, "If someone is listening to our conversation it is entirely inappropriate. If an investigation were needed, it would be inappropriate and probably illegal to even consider information from such undisclosed surveillance. It would be such surveillance that should be investigated."

He thought he heard a click on the telephone, but then wondered if he had imagined it. Was the situation affecting him, too? Was he displaying paranoia or was he demonstrating due caution? Would the U.S. Constitution support demands for a loyalty salute in one's own home?

Doctor Harvey concluded by saying, "I am concerned about what is happening. Please let me know if there is something I can do to help you and your family. Perhaps I could talk to an attorney here in Forsyth to see if there are legal steps for you to consider?"

Herman Mueller replied sternly, "Bitte, do not involve an attorney. I would not want to ask an attorney to risk being treated the way Judge Crum was treated. I appreciate your call and your concern. I think it will be best now for me to wait to see if the League wants any more from me. This war will not go on forever. I should tend to chores now. Vielen Dank for your call."

"Thank you for talking with me," replied Doctor Harvey.

There was a distinct click when Herman hung up the phone.

During the remainder of the morning as he saw patients, he was preoccupied by the realization that his concerns had been justified. Previously he had wondered if misunderstandings could lead to hateful accusations. Now, however, he was recognizing a more malicious process with accusations escalating to threats. He wondered how the spread of such accusations could be contained. Trying to help an individual

patient with paranoid perceptions was difficult enough. Trying to miti-
gate the spread of such perceptions in a community seemed beyond the
disease-control steps of which he was aware.

Later that afternoon, after the last scheduled patient had left, he sat at
his desk. He made notes in the records of patients he had seen. He noticed an unopened envelope May had placed on his desk earlier that day.

The envelope was addressed to Kelly K. Harvey, MD, County Health
Officer, Forsyth, Montana. It came from the State Board of Health. He
sliced open the envelope with a folding pocketknife he called his real
Barlow. He kept the knife in a drawer of his desk. He removed a letter. It
was signed by William F. Cogswell, MD, Secretary of the Board of Health.

The letter was to all county health officers in Montana and listed sev-
en emergency regulations for the control of Spanish influenza. Doctor
Cogswell anticipated the State Board of Health would enact these at
its October meeting. He wanted to be sure county health officers were
aware of these rules and encouraged implementation immediately.

The emergency regulations were:
1. Spanish influenza is hereby declared to be infectious, contagious,
   and communicable and dangerous to public health.
2. All patients suffering from influenza must be reported to the local or county health officer as soon as the diagnosis is made. Local
   and county health officers shall make a written report to the State
   Health Department Saturday night of each week of cases reported
   to them during the week. They shall report by wire any unusual
   outbreak of the disease.
3. When Spanish influenza appears in epidemic form in any community, the health officer having jurisdiction shall close the schools and
   prohibit all public gatherings.
4. Patients suffering from Spanish influenza shall be isolated as completely as possible until recovery. They shall be prohibited from any
   public gathering and from traveling on any common carrier.
5. When treated in hospital wards, patients suffering from Spanish
   influenza should be screened from other patients.
6. All discharges from nose and mouth of patients should be disin-
   fected at once.

7. On recovery or death, room or rooms in which patient lived while sick must be thoroughly cleaned; clothing and bedding used by patient must be hung in the open air at least two hours.

In recent issues of the *Journal of the American Medical Association* he had read accounts of severe illness being caused by influenza and how quickly illness had spread in parts of Europe and in some U.S. cities. The Cogswell letter made the danger seem clear although not yet present. He recognized the need to get this message to other physicians in the county, and to the commissioners, Sheriff Starr, school officials, and the public. He felt uneasy. He knew he would need to try to control this epidemic and to be prepared to comply with the emergency regulations.

CHAPTER THIRTEEN

October 1918

The events of September had been disturbing. Doctor Harvey thought, *Surely October will be a time for reconciliation.*

But now he was reconsidering. The gathering at the railway station this morning had not been a healing experience. During the last week of September, trials had been convened at the courthouse for six persons accused of sedition. Four were found guilty and sentenced to serve a prison term at the state penitentiary. This morning two of these men were delivered to the railway station and loaded onto a Northern Pacific car to be escorted to Deer Lodge. He had watched the gathering from across the street feeling much more remorse than reconciliation. This October day he hoped would be a day for future generations to remember but not repeat.

He was in his office reviewing neatly written messages May had placed on his desk. A mother was not able to bring her son to an appointment this afternoon because both she and the nine-year-old boy were too ill to come to town. Both had fever and fatigue. He spoke softly to himself, "Likely best for them to stay home. Good chance they have influenza. Best not to expose others. Need to confirm someone is available to help with food, water, chores."

He thought about how patients like these might benefit from being in a hospital for several days, but since there was no hospital in Forsyth he did not dwell on this thought.

Another message described a telephone call from the State Health

Department: how many cases of influenza had been reported last week? Doctor Harvey had delayed a report to the state because he had not received reports from other physicians. He suspected he was not the only physician seeing influenza-like illnesses, so he had asked May to contact each physician office in the county to encourage reporting and to confirm the tally for last week. He would talk with May in a few minutes to hear what she had learned.

He looked at the final message placed on his desk. Gerde had called to ask him to visit the Mueller ranch as soon as possible. Herman Mueller was very sick, as were two of the children. He knew the proud, self-reliant rancher must be very ill for Gerde to be allowed to call for help. Earlier that day he had taken some solace knowing Herman was not among the men being transported to Deer Lodge, but now a new concern moved in.

He walked to the examination room door and saw May had returned from lunch.

He said, "Thank you for the messages. Some of the illness is probably influenza. Would you please call the Mueller home and tell Gerde I will come to their ranch later this afternoon?"

"Yes, I will call," said May. "You have patients scheduled until four, so I'll tell Gerde it will probably be after five before you get there."

A young mother carrying her toddler son entered the office. The small boy sneezed but did not move his head from his mother's shoulder. The listless boy was too tired to move his arms or legs. The mother also sneezed. She blew her nose into a handkerchief she had just used to wipe her son's nose.

She said, "Hello, Doctor. Sorry I am late. It has not been easy to get my son dressed and out of the house today."

"Don't be concerned about the time. Please come in," he replied as he accompanied her to the examination room. She sat in the chair beside his desk with the boy's head still on her shoulder.

"I'll be back in just a minute," he said before returning to the entry area to talk with May.

"We need to review our triage procedures to identify patients with upper respiratory signs and fever as soon as possible and keep those patients away from other patients," he said. "Have you been able to contact physician offices to determine how many influenza cases have been seen? Also would you please contact Frances Olson and a county commissioner to arrange a time I could meet with each, preferably the three of us meeting together?"

May replied, "Yes. I will contact Frances and a commissioner. I have contacted the other physicians in the county; all have seen influenza cases. I have written the number of diagnosed cases from each office here."

She handed the note to him and continued. "I would very much like to review the triage procedures."

"Thanks and we shall," he said before stepping back into the examination room.

"When did your boy become ill?" he asked.

"Three days ago he got up in the morning and seemed to be fine. By afternoon he was sick, curled up in his bed, would not eat lunch," she said. "His forehead was very warm so I tucked him under the covers. The next day he started sneezing. Now I am not feeling well."

She sneezed again and wiped her nose with the same handkerchief.

He asked, "How old is he?"

"Twenty-three months."

"Do you have other children? Is anyone else in the family ill now?"

"My other children are six and eight years old. They are at school today and have not been ill. This morning my husband told me he was not feeling well, but he went out to tend to our animals. He has stayed outside working today."

He took the boy's temperature then wiped alcohol on the thermometer before checking the mother's. The boy's temperature was 102 degrees Fahrenheit and the mother's 100. He used his stethoscope to listen for breath sounds on the boy's back and then on the mother's. Both were breathing freely. He advised the mother to put the boy to bed, keep other family members away from him and away from her, too, as much as possible. And both of them should drink lots of fluids. He told her the illness was most likely influenza and would probably resolve within five to seven days.

The next two patients he saw had come for regular checkups of their medical conditions. One was a woman aged sixty-two who had intermittent urine incontinence and a prolapsed uterus for which he had prescribed a pessary when he had seen her about six weeks previously. The incontinence had not fully resolved but she said the frequency had decreased. He advised continuing use of the pessary.

The second patient was a railroad worker aged thirty-five who had sustained a deep laceration of his right forearm at work last week. Doctor Harvey had cleaned and stitched the wound. He was pleased to see it was healing with no sign of infection. He advised leaving the stitches in place. He would remove them when the patient visited again in one more week.

He saw more patients as the day went on. The last scheduled patient had called May to cancel because the patient had a fever and just wanted to go to bed. When May told him of this cancellation she said, "Influenza season does seem to be here. I do not recall visit cancellations like this happening so often last year."

He replied, "Yes, some of the patients seem to be quite ill. Would you please purchase an additional supply of facemasks at the pharmacy before it closes this afternoon? We will begin asking those with fever and cough to wear a mask while they are here. You and I may begin wearing facemasks, too. We will talk more about triage procedures tomorrow morning."

She responded, "I'll go to the pharmacy now. I did contact the commissioner and Frances Olson. They will both come here at 9:00 a.m. tomorrow morning."

Thank you for making that appointment so quickly," he said. "I am going to visit the Mueller ranch now."

During the drive to the Mueller ranch he felt increasingly uncomfortable about the crescendo of illnesses very likely due to influenza. He saw a few clouds in the distant western sky but above him the sky was clear. By the time he returned to town, he would be able to see an array of stars. He had long been fascinated by mythology—the propensity of people to explain the unknown by attributing influence to gods and stars. He anticipated sighting Aquarius, the water bearer, and maybe Pegasus, the horse god. In ancient times a flood such as the Yellowstone River deluge in June might have been attributed to an overactive Aquarius. And the designation of a horse god recognized essential contributions of horses to developing civilization century after century.

Even now in rural areas such as Rosebud County, horses remained essential to ranchers. Machines were increasingly used as substitutes for horses but were still measured by horsepower.

He wondered if his medical knowledge would be sufficient to control a deluge of illness once the influenza epidemic arrived in earnest. For centuries some diseases had been attributed to extraterrestrial influences. The term influenza was derived from a belief the illness was due to influence from the stars. He gave no credence to this archaic belief. He was convinced influenza was infectious. One prominent scientist had isolated a bacterium he thought to be the cause. He had filtered and grown this agent in the laboratory. Other scientists were not convinced. They thought the disease was caused by a yet to be identified agent so small it could not be filtered. In any event he could see the disease was highly communicable and for some patients life-threatening.

He continued driving west on River Valley Road until he turned onto the rutted, bumpy driveway and progressed slowly toward the Mueller's ranch house. Their border collie was now running beside the Hudson and barking, not threateningly, but as if to say, "Keep coming, this is the right direction."

When he parked the automobile near the house, Gerde came to greet him.

"Stille," she said to the obedient dog.

To Doctor Harvey she said, "Danke for coming. Mein Onkel ist very ill und die Kinder are also ill."

He responded, "Let's go inside so I can see them."

The house was single story. He entered into a combined kitchen and dining room and continued into the living room. A hallway led from the living room to three bedroom doors. Gerde guided him to one of the bedrooms where Herman was lying in bed. Jana Mueller sat in a chair beside the bed. She did not move when he entered the room. She was bent forward, her hands clasped in her lap, her face looking down at her hands. She did not speak.

He stepped to the bedside to examine Herman, whose face was ashen and cold to the touch. He was not breathing and had no pulse. Doctor Harvey judged he had been dead for an hour or more.

He looked at Gerde and said, "Let's take your aunt into the living room."

He took Jana's hand and said, "Please come with us. I am so sorry."

Gerde sat with her arm around Jana in the living room while Doctor Harvey returned to the bedroom. He covered Herman's face with the bedsheet before going to a second bedroom. There he found two young sisters lying beside each other in bed. He touched the forehead of each; neither felt febrile.

"How are you young women feeling?"

"We are feeling better today," replied one sister. The other nodded agreement.

Doctor Harvey examined them. Both were breathing easily and their lungs were clear to his stethoscope assessment.

He returned to the living room and asked Gerde if he could use the telephone. He called the funeral home and asked the mortician to come for the body. He also cautioned the mortician to have workers wear facemasks when handling the body.

He turned to Gerde, who was still sitting with Jana, and said, "It is very important for you to take care of yourself so you can care for the family at this time. Have you and the children eaten anything this afternoon? This would be a good time to prepare some food for them. Be sure they get lots of liquid to drink. I will stay until the funeral home workers come."

He sat beside Jana and said, "I am very sorry for your loss. Herman was a strong, loving man. Would you like me to contact the reverend at your church?"

She did not respond for what seemed like a long time but finally said very softly, "Ja, but we must sing a hymn auf Deutsch at the funeral." Then she cried and he put his arm around her as she leaned on him.

After Gerde had given some food to the ill children she returned to sit by Jana. Doctor Harvey called the reverend who said he, too, would visit the Mueller home that night.

About an hour passed before two men from the funeral home arrived. They wore facemasks while they put Herman Mueller into a body bag and carried it from the bedroom to their vehicle. One of the men talked with Gerde briefly about some aspects of handling and preparing the body. He agreed to call the next day to discuss plans for a funeral.

The other man mentioned to Doctor Harvey that this was the second body they had picked up this week for which a physician had advised them to wear a facemask. He asked if they would need more facemasks. Doctor Harvey explained influenza seemed to be spreading and more facemask use was likely.

Doctor Harvey realized there had become an urgent need to provide recommendations not just to funeral home workers but also to public safety workers and others in the community.

Before leaving the Mueller home he encouraged Gerde and Jana Mueller to get some sleep if they could. He also asked them not to hesitate to contact him if there was any way he might help. Gerde had tears in her eyes. Jana was not crying but had a distant, deeply pained look.

He felt solemn during the drive back to town. The North Star was clearly visible. While he knew it was not responsible for influenza, its appearance to commemorate the loss of Herman Mueller seemed appropriate. He knew many more commemorations would be needed before this epidemic ran its course.

In his room that evening he ate little; he had little hunger for food. He kept thinking about how little he had to offer those sick with influenza. Someday medicine might be more helpful for those suffering from this illness. Someday a vaccine might be developed to prevent the disease. But someday was not now.

He poured Flying U into a glass and closed his eyes. He saw his wife so vividly that for a moment he felt she was with him. Then he realized he was alone. He sipped the whiskey.

The next morning he washed his face and shaved using water in the white metal basin sitting atop the chest of drawers next to his bed. As he pulled on his shoes he saw the empty whiskey bottle on the table. What was he doing? He regularly advised patients not to drink excessively yet he, himself, regularly did. He resolved to cut back but also made a mental note to get another bottle of the Choisser brand later today.

When he arrived at his office, he called the funeral home to confirm the mortician was wearing a facemask when he prepared bodies. He was reassured when he heard use of facemasks was standard practice in all cases whether or not an infectious disease was the presumed cause of death.

Part of the mortician's reply startled him. "I received another call this morning to come for a body at a home here in town. The family's doctor thinks this death might be due to influenza. Then Sheriff Starr called. He said he would be calling you, too."

Doctor Harvey said, "I have not talked to the sheriff yet. What did he tell you?"

"He said he had been contacted by a rancher out on the Reservation Creek Road. The rancher had not seen his neighbors for a few days and went over to visit," continued the mortician. "Two neighbors were dead in their beds—a grandfather and his teenage grandson who had been staying with him to help with the livestock. Only a young granddaughter who had been helping with household work was alive. She was lying on a bed too ill to get up to help herself or the others. I'll be going for those bodies later this morning."

Doctor Harvey replied, "Oh my. Be sure your workers wear facemasks and wash their hands after handling the bodies. Thank you for this information."

Doctor Harvey called Harold Starr, who immediately said, "I was about to call you."

Harold recounted the events as the mortician had. Before ending the phone call, Doctor Harvey shared some information with Harold.

"This morning I will meet with a county commissioner regarding isolation and quarantine steps we may need to impose," he said. "You may be hearing from the commissioner about these issues soon."

"Thank you for calling," concluded Harold.

By the time he disconnected the phone call, May had come into the examination room. "The commissioner and Frances Olson are here. Shall I bring them in?"

"Yes, please," he said.

Once the commissioner and Frances were seated he said, "Thank you for coming. As you know an epidemic of Spanish influenza is sweeping through many parts of the country. I want to be sure you know the epidemic has arrived here and is likely to amplify during coming weeks. Some steps must be taken to try to limit the spread of disease and save some lives."

The commissioner did not seem surprised. He asked, "What steps do you recommend? To capture people's attention we will be competing with news and concerns about the war."

Doctor Harvey responded, "When family members and nearby neighbors are ill with influenza—some dying—the control measures will be of interest to many. Some of the measures will cause inconveniences. I think it will be possible to capture attention."

Frances observed, "Schools have been closed in Bozeman, Scobey, and several other towns already. Do we need to close schools here?"

"Yes. I think the schools should be closed until the epidemic subsides," he replied. "That will be more effective than trying to enforce quarantine measures each time a student develops influenza."

He continued, "It might be helpful for me to list the prevention steps we need to take. Then we can discuss individual steps as thoroughly as necessary. Listing these steps will take several minutes."

Both the commissioner and Frances nodded in agreement.

He began, "What I am recommending is based on advice from the State Health Department. Doctor Cogswell has sought information from the U.S. Public Health Service and communicable disease experts around the country. There is no surefire way to stop this influenza, but we can take steps to slow it down, to prevent some cases, and to save some lives."

Frances interrupted, "I read in the *Times-Journal* about a mail order product said to protect against influenza. At the school superintendents' meeting in Helena last month I heard there was a vaccine. Will we use these products?"

Doctor Harvey replied, "Well if the nostrums advertised in newspapers provided even half the benefit claimed I would be out of business. It would be good for the town if disease could be treated and prevented so easily, but I won't be without work anytime soon. Claims like those you have seen are entirely bogus. There is no evidence to support treatment with those products."

He paused briefly and continued, "And, no effective vaccine is available. A research physician in Pennsylvania, Doctor Lewis, thinks influenza is caused by bacteria, which some call Pfeiffer's bacillus. He has prepared a vaccine from the bacteria, but there is no evidence at this time the vaccine provides protection. The State Health Department is not recommending it.

Some of the illnesses with fever we saw during the spring may have been cases of influenza, but illness then was mild compared to what we're seeing now. This is a severe disease. It has a sudden onset and for some patients a rapid decline. The State Health Department says the disease hit hard in Scobey a couple weeks ago, then in Glendive, Great Falls, and some larger towns. It is here now and here are the steps we need to take.

"First, because the illness is passed from one person to another, assemblies of people need to be restricted. This means closing schools and restricting gatherings at places people congregate including saloons, churches, and fraternal organizations. I realize we can't shut down businesses such as mercantile stores, barbershops, or banks, but we need to advise business owners not to let crowds form in their establishments. People should not be in stores or shops any longer than necessary.

"Second, public safety personnel including police and funeral home workers should wear facemasks to protect themselves. Store clerks, barbers, deliverymen, and others who work with the public should also wear facemasks while they are working.

"Also, the Board of Commissioners should appoint a quarantine warden who could help Sheriff Starr enforce health ordinance requirements such as these. A warden could post notices, identify and report to me cases consistent with influenza, and report to the sheriff if a person who lives in a house where there is an influenza case breaks quarantine rules and lingers in public. I do not know what funds might be used to support a quarantine warden, but I strongly recommend establishing this temporary position for two or three months.

"I will be reporting the number of influenza cases to the State Health Department each week. I will work with physicians in the county to ensure families of diagnosed cases are advised about the importance of isolation and quarantine."

Doctor Harvey poured water into glasses for himself, the commissioner, and Frances. Then he went on.

"It is likely many will be ill in coming weeks. Some of the ill would benefit from care at a hospital. Since we do not have a hospital, we should establish a hospital-like setting soon.

"Doctor Cogswell has formed a cadre of physicians who are

providing assistance to rural areas of the state. Six of these physicians have been assigned to work in Montana by the U.S. Public Health Service. If one were to come to Forsyth he would be working in a military uniform. Another physician in this cadre is Doctor Lanstrum from Helena. As you know he has been a candidate for the U.S. Senate seat, but he has suspended his campaign to be involved in the statewide influenza control effort."

At this mention the commissioner interrupted.

"Hell," he said. "Lanstrum may be well intended and may provide useful service around the state. But, if you ask me he suspended his campaign because Tom Walsh is so far ahead. Lanstrum has no chance to win in any event. If the current administration wants to stop the spread of influenza, why are they holding a political gathering in Bozeman despite their own advice against public gatherings? That kind of stunt doesn't add credibility to the kind of restrictions we may be establishing in Rosebud County. Damned Democrats in Helena— a house of duplicity!"

Doctor Harvey was aware of the issues that piqued the commissioner's ire but opted not to comment further on them.

Instead he asked the commissioner, "Would you be willing to convene a meeting of the commissioners soon to discuss, and I hope enact, a health ordinance based on the recommendations I am making?"

The commissioner replied, "Yes. When could you have the recommendations in written form for us to consider at a meeting? We'll meet as soon as the document is ready to review."

He replied, "I'll prepare the recommendations this evening. You will have them tomorrow."

The commissioner responded, "Good. It won't be easy to keep the commissioners' and town's attention on disease control with the war and the draft and all the Loyalty League activity continuing, to say nothing of decisions for distributing funds for the grain seed support program. Still, we should enact the health ordinance soon."

Frances added, "Montana State College has suspended all its classes for this term. One of our local high school graduates has been studying nursing at MSC and the Deaconess Hospital in Bozeman. She decided to return to Forsyth to be with her family until classes resume. She might be a candidate to help provide nursing care here if a temporary hospital is established."

"That is a good idea," he replied. "I would like to talk with this young woman. Would you please leave her name with May?"

"Yes, I will," said Frances. "When will we meet to confirm procedures for closing schools as a result of this health ordinance?"

"Let's meet tomorrow," he said. "I'll provide written recommendations to the commissioner and bring a copy to your office. I'd like to do this before noon. Would you be available tomorrow at eleven?"

She replied, "Yes. I will be at my office. Thank you for the briefing today and for the work you are doing."

The commissioner added, "Thank you indeed. I'll see you tomorrow morning."

After the commissioner and Frances left, he asked May to reschedule the next day's morning appointments. He told her he would have handwritten recommendations when he came to the office and asked that she type the text so he could provide a clear, professional-looking document to the commissioner.

May said, "I'll clear the schedule and be ready to type. This will give me a chance to use a new ribbon and try the new box of carbon paper, too. My Underwood can provide a professional-looking original. Then I'll type another copy with some extra carbon copies you may be able to use."

"Thank you," he said. "You are invaluable, you know!"

While he prepared the list of recommendations that evening, he felt more involved with the public's health than he had since arriving almost two years ago. Still, he could not displace a sense of foreboding about persisting allegations of sedition or the burst of influenza already underway.

CHAPTER FOURTEEN

November 21, 1918

Doctor Harvey sat by the table in his room at the Alexander Hotel Annex. The sun was not up yet. He sipped the stale coffee he had just reheated. For nearly an hour he recalled the events of the last three weeks.

The night before, he had made rounds at the Masonic Lodge until eleven. The temperature outside had dipped to fourteen degrees below zero. The Lodge had begun serving as a temporary hospital that week. All fourteen patients there had influenza—male patients in the Forsyth Club room in the front of the building and women in the Masonic Lodge room in the rear. The patients were lying on cots, separated one from another by sheets hung like screens. A Red Cross nurse was in charge of staffing. Doctor Harvey had reviewed the status of each patient with the nurse serving the evening shift. He had also talked with the young nursing student who was home in Forsyth because her college in Bozeman had suspended classes due to the influenza outbreak. He knew nursing care was the most important service a hospital could offer during this epidemic. Not every small community would find nurses, in part because so many were serving at military facilities in the United States and in Europe. He wanted to support the brave nurses who were available and working every day at the emergency hospital.

This was the second emergency hospital established in Forsyth to provide care for influenza patients otherwise unable to have the supportive care they needed. The first had been the Marcy School, converted into a hospital in mid-October after the other schools had been closed to help prevent the spread of influenza. Three weeks later the Forsyth school superintendent, to whom city officials had assigned responsibility to determine when schools could be reopened, had decided the epidemic was abating. So all schools were opened again. However, they were open for only a day before they were once again closed. The influenza case count had resurged over the weekend preceding school opening. The Masonic Lodge became the emergency hospital site in place of the briefly opened Marcy School.

He recognized that the steps taken to control the spread of the disease had been overwhelmed by an onslaught of infections but also by inadequately coordinated prevention steps. In early October, while he was discussing quarantine procedures with county commissioners and Frances Olson, the county school superintendent, another Forsyth physician, serving as the city health officer, had been discussing potential quarantine steps with the mayor, city aldermen, and the city school superintendent. During the second week of October, fifty cases of influenza were reported in the city and more from the county. Then the need to proceed with the State Board of Health recommendations seemed obvious in both the city and the county. On a Saturday, orders were issued to close all picture shows, lodge meetings, and public gatherings. Schools in both the city and county were closed the following Monday for an indefinite period. The superintendents were designated responsible to determine when schools would be opened again.

During the third week of October, more than 100 cases were reported in the city, and twelve residents in or near Forsyth died of influenza. Only then, with urging from Sheriff Starr and essential support from the Red Cross and the Rosebud County Council of Defense, had the emergency hospital been established at the Marcy School. The next week more than 200 cases were reported from the city and at least thirty patients with influenza were in the care of volunteer nurses at the emergency hospital. Parents were urged to see to it their children stayed off the main streets. There were no bewitching parties or trick-or-treating on Halloween.

Doctor Harvey took another sip of his coffee and continued to recall the recent events, especially the way quarantine steps had been interpreted and implemented. Although both the city aldermen and the county commissioners supported restrictions on public gatherings, not all gatherings were equally restricted. Exceptions soon arose. Whether to restrict gatherings at saloons generated considerable dissent. He heard a spectrum of the disagreement from his patients during many October office visits.

One saloon owner came for medical attention because he had noticed a yellowish tint to his skin. However, he was more interested in talking about the restriction of gatherings at his saloon than his health. He argued reasonable consumption of liquor was more beneficial than taking too much medicine for illness such as the flu. He claimed this was a fact because he had read in a newspaper that the mayor of Butte had made this assertion. He railed against too much regulation but had accommodated to the restriction in Forsyth, which allowed saloons to sell liquor by the package for consumption elsewhere but not to sell individual drinks to be consumed at the saloon.

Another patient, a leader of the Women's Christian Temperance Union, spent time with Doctor Harvey castigating aldermen and commissioners for bowing to the interests of demon rum. She argued that an ordinance should simply close saloons now since Montana's state prohibition law would close them beginning December 31 that year anyway. "Better," she said, "to stop all sales than begin a practice of package liquor sales." Yet another patient declared, "Beer is a German beverage" and that should be enough reason to ban its sale. Finally a reverend who came to the office because of persistent headaches objected to an exception for saloons because the ordinance prohibited all Sunday and other church services.

He was asked repeatedly about the use of facemasks to decrease the spread of infection. Although he had advised use to many who had regular contact with the public, he also had lingering doubt about the efficacy of mask use. He thought that facemasks might be helpful, and they probably did not harm, so he would recommend them. Still he also wondered if users might develop a false sense of security and get closer to other people, potentially infected people, than they would have if not wearing a mask. Although gauze masks had been distributed preferentially to military sites, Red Cross workers in Rosebud County made special effort to provide for local demand. He had advised healthcare workers and others to clean the gauze facemasks with an antiseptic each day if the masks were to be reused.

He read in the November 7 issue of the *Times-Journal* about the "easy victory" of Republicans, both locally and statewide, in the 1918 elections. He also read the premature United Press report that "Germany surrenders," but on November 11 he learned an armistice had been established. This news led Sheriff Starr to call him.

Harold asked, "Have you heard? The war is over."

"Yes, I just learned," he replied. "This is great news."

Harold continued, "A group is gathering at the saloon already with a plan to celebrate. It's easy to understand the motivation, plus it's cold outside today. However, they are clearly violating the health ordinance. I'm calling to ask your opinion. Should we let this celebration go on? The gathering would likely grow in numbers and go into the night. Or, should we try to end this before it expands to other parts of town?"

He contemplated this extraordinary situation then asked, "If you were to close the saloon this afternoon, do you think this gathering would end or simply move elsewhere?"

Harold responded, "It would move elsewhere. I think there is a hunger to celebrate this news."

"There may also be a desire to have drinks at the saloon at least one more time before the state prohibition takes effect in about six weeks," observed Doctor Harvey. "Everything considered, it might be best to advise the saloon owner the health ordinance remains in effect and he should not sell drinks by the glass. However, if patrons who have purchased packaged liquor linger at the saloon in celebration of the end of the war, the ordinance will not be strictly enforced for this night only."

Harold responded, "I was hoping you would make a suggestion such as that. I'm not so sure we could stop a gathering to celebrate war's end, and I'm not so sure I'd want to try. We'll get back to strict enforcement tomorrow."

Doctor Harvey said, "We may regret this if the influenza case count jumps after a few days, but trying to put a lid on this celebration doesn't seem like the right thing to try."

He paused before continuing, "Have you heard any discussion yet of a parade or other community events to mark the end of the war?"

"Haven't heard anyone talking about a parade yet," said Harold. "That will probably come."

"My advice would be to delay an organized parade until the influenza epidemic dies down," said Doctor Harvey. "I hope this will be soon, but the number of cases reported each week is still growing."

Harold said, "We may need to cross that bridge before long. The commissioners will have the last say on the parade issue. For now I'll ask my quarantine warden to advise the saloon owner as you suggested, but not to join in the gathering. Wouldn't look right for the quarantine warden to do that. Thanks for the advice, Doc."

Then in what seemed like an afterthought to Doctor Harvey, Harold continued. "By the way, I was sorry to hear Herman Mueller died. I understand no funeral service was organized, but the family and friends gathered at his graveside and sang his favorite hymns in German. Maybe the end of this war will get everyone to ease off a bit. Haven't heard what might happen with the Loyalty League. Wouldn't seem right to trouble this family any more."

As Doctor Harvey replied, "No, it doesn't seem right," he heard a click at the other end of the telephone line. He didn't know if Harold had disconnected before hearing his remark.

As he finished his morning coffee, there was a purposeful knock on the door of his room. He knew the knock, and the purpose. He opened the door and saw an eleven-year-old boy, the son of the hotel owners.

The previous week a hotel guest who had appeared ill when he checked in had not checked out two days later on his scheduled departure date. A housekeeper had gone to clean the room and found the guest in bed, dead. After examining the body, Doctor Harvey concluded this man had most likely died of influenza. Since then the hotel owners had had their son knock on the door of each occupied room each morning around 7:00 a.m. A voice from within the room or an opened door would verify an occupant was alive. The boy would then move to the next room. If there was no response, the boy would contact his parents, who would investigate further.

"Good morning, Doctor," the boy greeted. "All the guests have responded today. Now I can do my other chores. Do you know how much longer the school will be closed?"

"I appreciate everything you are doing," replied Doctor Harvey. "School will open again as soon as the influenza is under control, but I can't be sure yet when that will be."

The boy frowned, turned, and walked to the stairs.

Doctor Harvey placed the coffee cup on the counter, washed his face, donned his heavy winter coat in preparation for another chilly November day, and walked to his office. In the late afternoon he would again make rounds to review the status of patients at the Masonic Lodge.

One of the scheduled patients was a seventy-three-year-old woman who had severely swollen ankles and shortness of breath after taking only a few steps. He wondered how she had managed to get to his office from her home almost six blocks away. He asked, "Is your husband with you today?"

She replied, "Yes. He brought me in the wheelchair you helped us get last month. He's getting some groceries at the store while I am here. Then we will roll back home again. Someday someone will put motors on these wheelchairs. Then folks like me won't be so much trouble to others."

"I doubt your husband feels bothered by helping you," he replied. "How long have you two been married?"

She smiled and said, "It was fifty-five years in August. I reckon we've grown accustomed to having each other around."

He paused briefly and asked, "What brought you for a visit today?"

"Well, the wheelchair did!" she replied and smiled slyly. "But I came because I need more of those digitalis pills for my dropsy."

He smiled broadly. "Let me listen to your heart first."

He placed the earpieces of his stethoscope into his ears and examined her heart and lungs. Then he said, "It's a good idea to keep taking digitalis. It helps your heart beat stronger. I'll prepare a prescription so you and your husband can get more at the pharmacy."

He walked beside her as she slowly shuffled from the examination room into the entry area of the office. He saw her husband and the wheelchair waiting. He asked, "How are you doing?"

The husband replied in a deep, resonant voice, "I'm doin' fine thank you. As long as I can stay away from the grippe I'll have no complaints."

After the couple left he asked May, "Did she tell you how long they've been married?"

May said, "Fifty-five years! Her husband was just telling me about the party they had in August. Their children, grandchildren, and neighbors helped them celebrate."

He observed, "Looks like they have both grown accustomed to having each other around."

That afternoon between patient visits he thought about the war ending—and wondered if the war's side effects would ever end. Because the draft had been cancelled, men like himself, whose draft number had been called recently, probably would not be called to duty. The killing and carnage in Europe was over, but the wounded and disabled would need services for years. Young men would be returning to Rosebud County and some would be among the wounded and disabled. Would the intense suspicion and animosity toward persons with German heritage finally abate?

Before he left his office he reviewed reports from the funeral home, the county clerk, and the quarantine warden. The war was over, but the influenza siege was going strong. As he left his office, he said to May, "At least the red horse will stop supporting the pale horse now."

May did not know what he meant by this, but he was gone before she could ask.

He walked to the Masonic Lodge to conduct rounds. He suspected some of the patients he saw there would be included in the next death reports he received from the funeral home and the county clerk's office.

In his room at the Alexander Hotel Annex that evening, his thoughts were focused on disease and medicine. If his efforts were worthwhile, why had he not been able to do more for the patients at the temporary hospital? Or the older woman with dropsy? Or the rail-thin boy age twelve with diabetes whose mother was at her wits' end trying to comply with the diet instructions she had been given for her son? Or other patients whose diseases seemed to be a step ahead of his therapeutic armamentarium? Why was his wife not here? Why was their baby not now a thriving three year old?

He felt the familiar pain return. When he awoke the next morning, another empty bottle of Flying U sat beside his bed.

CHAPTER FIFTEEN

November 27, 1918

Tomorrow was Thanksgiving Day. Doctor Harvey was looking forward to dinner with May and her family; she'd invited him to share their meal and giving of thanks.

That morning he'd driven his Hudson south on Reservation Creek Road. It was covered by an overnight dusting of snow, the first snowfall of the season. The temperature was twenty degrees Fahrenheit when he left town, but it felt colder here as he drove very slowly to avoid sliding into the ditch. The landscape was beautiful: snow-covered fields lay on each side of the road, pine trees on "the bench"—what locals ranchers called the plateau—stood like sentinels watching over the land, and leafless trees lined the creek for which the road was named.

He imagined Crow and Sioux on horseback riding in this area in the days before the steamboats and railroads brought thousands to their country—before much of the land was taken from them through brute force and disease, before roads brought swift-moving, horseless carriages, when horseback riders would see and feel the majestic beauty of the land in ways drivers like him missed by passing through too quickly.

As he pulled his coat more tightly against his body, he marveled at how the Crow, Sioux, Northern Cheyenne, and other tribes had survived the short days and long nights of winter on these high plains, when temperatures were much colder than the still-above-zero chill he was bundled up against.

Cattle congregated in a field on the east side of the road. They were clustered together, side-to-side, in small groups of eight to ten. The exhaled breath of each formed a cloud that rose eight to ten inches over their nostrils before disappearing. These clouds looked like smoke puffed from steam engines. The cattle nuzzled the ground in search of grass—easier to find in April and May when these fields were covered by the annual miracle of a regenerated landscape.

This was the first time Doctor Harvey had been away from town—and the influenza ward at the Masonic Lodge—in more than three weeks. He was so lost in thought he did not notice a rider on horseback beside the road until just a few feet away. The rider gestured for him to stop. He recognized the local rancher and slowed to a stop.

"Doctor Harvey, I thought it might be you," said the warmly bundled rider. "Not many Hudson automobiles make it out this way even when the weather is good. Where are you headed?"

Doctor Harvey replied, "Good to see you. I was just observing how beautiful this land is and feeling a little sorry for the cattle looking for a meal under the snow out there. I'm on my way to the Swensen's homestead to see how the mister is doing. He's been ill, might have influenza."

The rancher responded with a request. "My wife is also ill, maybe influenza, too. She hasn't been able to get out of bed for the last three days. Would you mind stopping at our place to see her?"

He replied, "I should be able to stop on my way back from the Swensen's this afternoon. I'll be happy to see her."

The rancher asked again, "Couldn't you see her now? She's very ill."

He responded, "Mrs. Swensen's message indicated her husband is also very ill. I'll be back in just a few hours to see your wife before I return to town."

"No, Doc," the rancher said. "You will see her now."

He pulled a Winchester rifle from the scabbard attached to his saddle and pointed the rifle at Doctor Harvey.

Doctor Harvey looked down the muzzle of the rifle. He had heard of a rancher in another county who had forced a physician at gunpoint to visit the rancher's home to see several ill family members. He had not heard whether or not there were repercussions for that rancher. The action sounded like kidnapping to him. Events such as this reflected the high level of anxiety many people were experiencing during the influenza epidemic. He had not anticipated this action in Rosebud County. He decided the best course of action for him was to see the rancher's wife now and then go to the Swensen home.

"You can put that rifle down. I'll see your wife. Would you like to get into the automobile and let your horse follow us down the driveway?"

The rancher responded, "No thank you, Doctor. I'll just ride behind your automobile."

He drove very carefully down the snow-covered driveway toward the two-story house about half a mile from Reservation Creek Road. He parked in front of the house next to a picketed area likely to be a flower garden in the spring. He carried his medical bag and walked with the rifle-carrying rancher into the house. The rancher instructed his two near-teenage sons to go to their room and stay there. They ascended the stairs without comment.

"She is over here," the rancher said and pointed to a room in one corner of the ground floor.

Doctor Harvey found her lying in bed. She was alert enough to answer questions but was very weak. She had been ill for six days. At first she had had fever, cough, and fatigue. Three days prior, the fatigue intensified and she began having trouble breathing. He took a thermometer from his bag and measured her temperature. It was only slightly elevated but her breathing was labored. With his stethoscope he heard little air moving into the left lung field. She had influenza with its most dangerous complication.

He said, "You have pneumonia. Have you been using any treatment?"

She spoke so softly he had to lean close to hear her response. "I have been taking cinnamon mixed with milk and putting cold towels on my forehead."

He was aware of these common remedy steps and wouldn't discourage them. At a hospital he would treat with supplemental oxygen by mask; at a large medical center he might provide antiserum, about which he had read. But here in rural Montana he could only offer aspirin to help keep her temperature down and provide some pain relief. He advised she should stay in bed, drink plenty of fluids, and eat regularly to regain her strength.

He concluded, "I need to get over to the Swensen home now."

"Oh. I hope no one there is ill," she said softly but with sincere concern.

As he neared the front door he heard the rancher say remorsefully, "Doctor, I am sorry I pulled my rifle on you. I hope you understand how worried I have been about my wife. Thank you for seeing her. How much should I pay you for this visit?"

He replied tersely, "I do understand how concerned everyone is about influenza. My assistant will contact you after Thanksgiving about payment for the visit."

The Hudson started after only two attempts with the starter. The driveway back to Reservation Creek Road was uphill, but the automobile traversed the incline despite some spinning of the tires.

About ten minutes later he turned down the Swensen's driveway and followed it to the top of the knoll, from which he could see their house in the small valley below. He decided to park on the knoll and walk the remaining distance downhill. He did not want to chance getting the Hudson stuck on the steep return to the knoll top.

It was now 12:30 p.m. The temperature had warmed a little, although it was still below freezing. Breathing the crisp, fresh air was invigorating. He proceeded down the driveway. The soles of his boots slipped a little with each step, requiring him to take short strides to avoid losing his balance.

He looked ahead. His destination was a small house in a narrow valley surrounded by the enormous, beautiful, but sometimes cruel land. He realized the chilled weather and snow-dusted ground was only a harbinger of the extreme temperatures and fence-post-topping snows winter would bring for months on end. He marveled at the homesteaders who could survive these conditions and thrive again when spring finally came. They would do this without electricity and without telephones. They would rely on the tenacity needed to hand-pump water from wells for themselves and their livestock, and to cut and split trees for wood to burn in potbelly stoves—which allowed huddled homesteader families to emerge from their homes unfrozen day after day to look winter in the eye and declare, "We are here to stay." He wondered how many of the homesteaders would achieve their here-to-stay goal as the years went by.

Coming up the driveway bounding and barking was Bingo. When the excited dog approached, Doctor Harvey removed the woolen glove on his left hand, reached forward palm-up, and said, "Hi, pal. Thanks for coming to greet me."

The dog sniffed his hand and came closer to brush his leg. He rubbed the top of the dog's head and back. Bingo seemed satisfied for the moment, then turned and began running back down the driveway. Doctor Harvey followed. Several minutes later they ascended the steps onto the porch to be greeted by Amanda Swensen.

"Doctor, I am so glad you came," she said. "Charles is very sick. He was not able to get out of bed yesterday and again today. Please come in."

"Let me see him," he said, slipping off his coat and gloves.

As he moved toward a back bedroom, he noticed Bingo had come into the house, too. He had lain beside Axel and Raymond, who were sitting near the stove. A crib placed a safe distance from the stove contained a bundle wrapped in a pink blanket, from which he heard babbling sounds.

He found Charles in bed. Like the rancher's wife he had seen earlier that day, Charles was responsive but weak, had labored breathing, and had a modestly elevated temperature. The stethoscope examination suggested pneumonia, the unfortunately common complication of influenza Doctor Harvey had seen again and again in recent weeks. He again provided aspirin and urged this patient to drink plenty of fluids and eat regularly.

He and Amanda returned to the living room to join the boys and Bingo near the stove.

"How have you boys been doing?" he asked.

They each said, "Fine." Neither elaborated but both appeared healthy. Both were wearing wool socks and heavy pullover sweaters.

He asked Amanda, "Did you make these beautiful sweaters? What a wonderful skill to have."

She looked pleased he had noticed the result of many hours of knitting. "Yes. It was nothing really."

He looked at the piano sitting in the living room. He remained impressed by the presence of a baby grand, just as he had been when he first visited this home. He said, "If I recall correctly you brought this lovely piano from Iowa. Would you play something for me?"

She went to the piano, lifted the keyboard cover, and began playing "Für Elise." She was accomplished; the diminished chords she played with her right hand were haunting. There was no concert hall within a hundred miles, yet he felt as if he were at one of the concerts he had attended regularly in Chicago.

He said, "Lovely. Beethoven would be very pleased to hear this."

She finished the melody and said, "I love this instrument and the music. I want to teach Helen to play when she is bigger. Then we will share music with each other just as we share the middle name Elizabeth. Maybe someday she will have a daughter with whom she can also share a middle name and music?"

He looked into the crib at the face of the sleeping baby, her head topped by a pink wool cap and body warmly bundled in one blanket and covered by another. He asked, "How is little Helen doing? She must be about fifteen months old now if I recall correctly?"

"Yes, fifteen months," Amanda replied. "She is doing well. I am keeping her away from Charles while he is ill. He misses her but I pray she does not get this terrible influenza."

Her tone shifted, and she asked, "Would you stay for dinner? I don't know how to thank you for coming on a day like this."

He declined the invitation, saying, "No, but thank you. Hearing the piano played so beautifully was worth the trip. I want to get back to town before dark."

He picked up his coat and gloves, which were warm from sitting near the stove. "I must be going."

As Doctor Harvey was preparing to leave, Axel stepped into his boots by the front door and put on his heavy coat, wool hat, and gloves. He said, "I'll walk with you to your automobile."

He turned back to his mother and said, "While I'm out there, I'll put hay in the mow for the cattle and bring more firewood into the house."

"Thank you, Axel," she said. "When you get back, Raymond will go with you to break the ice on the water trough in the barn and help pump more water for the animals."

She looked at Doctor Harvey and said, "Thank you so much for checking on Charles."

As the two made their way up the driveway, Bingo ran in large circles around them, occasionally coming close enough for a pat on the head and to jump up and lick Axel's face.

Doctor Harvey asked about the chores the two brothers did each day. Axel listed feeding and watering the cattle and chickens, cleaning the barn, cutting firewood, and shoveling a path to the outhouse if snow was deep. He also said his mother made sure they did school homework each day, too.

When they arrived at the crest of the knoll, Axel asked, "When will school start again? I'd like to see my friends and my teacher."

Doctor Harvey replied, "I don't know exactly when school will open again. It will be possible as soon as influenza stops spreading. I just don't know yet."

He got into his Hudson, turned the key, and pushed the starter once, twice, and on the third try the engine sputtered to a start. He pushed down on the gas pedal to race the engine and then let the engine run. Through the partly opened door, he thanked Axel for accompanying him. He secured the door, put the automobile in gear, and began a slow, careful drive back toward Reservation Creek Road.

As he turned onto the road, he looked back and waved at Axel, who then disappeared along with Bingo to walk back to the house—and to the chores awaiting him.

It was now nearly three in the afternoon. Despite the slick roads, he was confident he would get home before dark—granted he was not intercepted for another home visit. The temperature was beginning to fall. The crust of ice atop the snow remaining on the road crunched under the Firestone Cord tires. He reasoned that the lonely tire tracks he saw on the road ahead were probably the tracks he had left earlier that day. He held the steering wheel tightly with both hands mile after mile. At fifteen miles per hour, almost an hour passed before he reached the junction with River Valley Road, where he turned east toward town.

He thought, *If it were summer, with hours of daylight remaining, I would stop to see Gerde and her family. But now I need to complete the last five miles of today's journey and get to town while some daylight remains.* He turned on the Hudson's headlights.

A train whistle in the distance pierced the quiet; the afternoon westbound train had left the station. In recent weeks he had treated several railroad workers who had influenza. He had advised these men to stay away from work until their fever and cough resolved. This meant they would stay in town for a few days at the hotel, the Blue Front Boarding House, or, in one case, in a hospital bed at the Masonic Lodge. He wondered if railroad workers or passengers had brought influenza to Rosebud County. The workers were required to wear facemasks when interacting with the public, but he remained skeptical about the efficacy of the masks.

The role of the railroad system was evolving. It had been nationalized in December 1917 with the goal to make cargo transport more efficient, especially for carrying materials to support the war effort. He had read the nationalization could continue by law up to twenty-one months after the treaty had been signed, but he wondered how railroads would be affected by decreased crop yields due to persisting decreases in rainfall. Less demand and less supply of wheat and other crops could not be good for farmers and ranchers—or for the railroad. Still, many railroad workers would continue to need medical care for years to come.

As he parked near the Alexander Hotel he said to himself, "The fate of the railroads and the ranchers is too much to think about right now. I need to assess patients at the Masonic Lodge and also see if May left any messages for me."

He found that some patients at the temporary hospital were very ill but no patient had died for more than seventy-two hours. He decided responding to messages at his office could wait until tomorrow.

For supper he had a sandwich and coffee in his room at the Annex. Since the influenza epidemic arrived, he had stopped going to the café because he did not want to appear to be disregarding the public health ordinance he himself had recommended. He began reading a recent issue of the *Journal of the American Medical Association* but was soon asleep.

The next morning he heard a *knock, knock, knock* on the door. When he opened it he was greeted by the hotel owner's son. "All the guests have answered," the young man said. "No need to call the funeral home today."

Doctor Harvey was glad to learn this. However, it occurred to him if he had received such a message prior to October, he would have found the news trivial. Now though, the news brought relief and hope.

He went to the Masonic Lodge. No one had died there overnight either; however, no patient was well enough to be discharged that day. He thanked the nurse for working on Thanksgiving.

She replied, perhaps smiling under her gauze mask, "I enjoy working with patients while leaving all the meal preparation at home to my sister, her daughters, and my daughters. By the time I get home this evening a wonderful meal will be waiting for our families to celebrate together."

Next he went to his office to read messages. One was from the mortician, who wanted Doctor Harvey to know only one casket was available but more had been ordered. Another was from the State Board of Health and summarized the epidemic in Montana from the beginning of October through the first three weeks of November. The number of influenza deaths among American Indians on reservations, highlighted in the report, was particularly troubling to him. Another striking observation in the report was the marked increase in the number of cases reported during the week following November 11. He had sensed an increase in Rosebud County but had not taken the time to summarize the case reports May had collected.

Doctor Harvey had been concerned about the advice he had given Sheriff Starr and allowing relaxation of the prohibition of public gatherings. Had this facilitated a resurgence of influenza? The statewide data from the Board of Health suggested Armistice Day gatherings might have increased the spread of disease. Some cases might have been prevented by adherence to the ordinance. He was struck by the way reported disease information could be used to answer important disease control questions.

He considered the value of evidence from disease reporting not only for formulating public health ordinances but also for physicians and nurses to use in patient care. Years ago he had read about Florence Nightingale and how she collected information about illness in field hospitals during the Crimean War. She had used the information to improve conditions for ill and injured soldiers. He wondered how care in hospitals in Europe during the recently ended war had been influenced by recommendations made decades before by the Lady with the Lamp. Could systems for disease reporting be further improved or enhanced to support timely public health ordinances or more valuable treatment decisions?

He had read about a training program at Yale University School of Medicine to prepare physicians to work on public health issues. He planned to learn more about this program as he weighed whether or not to remain in Forsyth now that the war had ended.

From his office he walked the six blocks to May's home. He saw his exhaled breath condense before his face. He thought of the cattle breathing the cold air in their pasture yesterday, and their search for grass beneath the snow. His search for food was much easier. Once he entered May's home, the aroma from the turkey cooking in the oven instantly warmed him.

In the dining area between the kitchen and living room, a table was already set for eight: May's family, a neighbor's family, and himself. On the white linen tablecloth were place settings, each consisting of a china plate and china bread plate, a water glass with a red ribbon on the stem, a cup for coffee, a knife, a spoon, two forks, and a cloth napkin. Some food had already been placed on the table: mashed potatoes, pickles, aromatic bread rolls, orange slices, and fruitcake, along with containers of water and apple juice. Large platters with turkey and stuffing were being prepared in the kitchen. He could see pumpkin pies on the kitchen counter, too. The feast spread before him would surely be as delicious as it was meticulous.

The sight and the smell of this scene brought to mind his own family's Thanksgiving dinners during his childhood and adolescence. Since Marie died he had been so focused on his grief he had thought little about his family or about friends. As he realized this he resolved to call his brother later that day and to talk with him about his family and neighbors from their childhood.

Dinner was served, and the guests contrasted the royal treatment of this evening with wartime meals of recent years.

May's husband said, "This is a delicious departure from our Hooverized diets!"

He was alluding to the diet recommended by Herbert Hoover, head of the U.S. Food Administration, in order to provide humanitarian relief to Belgium and other areas in war-ravaged Europe. The slogan Food Wins Wars had accompanied wheatless Wednesdays, meatless Tuesdays, and porkless Thursdays in 1917 and 1918 in the United States.

After pumpkin pie with whipped cream, coffee, and then some brandy, Doctor Harvey thanked May for the wonderful afternoon. Rather than going directly to his room he stopped at his office to make telephone calls. Before phoning his brother, he called the Mueller family. He dialed and waited for an answer.

"Hello," said a voice he recognized.

"Hello. Is this Gerde?" he responded. "This is Doctor Harvey. I hope you have had a wonderful Thanksgiving."

After a long pause, he repeated, "Is this Gerde?"

"Ja," came the voice on the telephone. "This ist Gerde. Danke, thank you, for calling. We have had a good dinner. The Reverend and his Frau brought food to us. But we are nicht wunderbar." Her voice had faded to silence and he had a feeling she was about to cry.

He knew the family was having a very difficult time since Mr. Mueller died. He had heard that members of their church congregation had been visiting and helping with work at the ranch. He asked, "Do you have a few moments to talk? Is there something I can do to help?"

Another long pause followed.

"It is sehr schwer. Frau Mueller is sehr traurig. She sits and looks out the window. She does not talk, even to die Kinder. I try to help. I cook and keep the house clean. Die Kinder also help. It is hard for them. We have eggs and milk, eggs from unseren Hühnern and milk from unseren Kühen," came the effusive answer from Gerde, who seemed to be relieved by sharing this information.

But as she continued the momentary relief he had sensed turned to despair, "Yesterday we received zwei sehr schwer letters. I do not know what we will do."

"Can you tell me about these letters?" he asked.

"Ja," she said. "It is sehr schwer; sehr schwer for all of us."

She began to cry but managed to continue, "One letter is from the bank. Das loan Herr Mueller used to buy wheat seed and fertilizer must be paid. The $600 has not been paid yet. The loan has been fore-closed. We will need to find a way to pay it. But that is not the worst news we received."

She was sobbing.

He could tell she was distraught. He talked while she cried, "I am very sorry to learn of this foreclosure notice. It is very insensitive of the bank to pursue this at the time your family is grieving—and at a time we are all asked to give thanks for blessings and mercy and an end to sorrow and great peril. And you received worse news than this?"

Gerde had composed herself enough to describe the second letter. She began, "Meine Schwester wrote the letter more than drei weeks ago. The letter finally came. Meine Mutter ist dead."

She was crying again but continued, "She died in October. She had fever from typhus. The war has been sehr schwer. Now meine Schwester and Bruder have nothing. I must find a way to be with them, for them to come here. But we have trouble here, too. Es ist sehr, sehr schwer."

He did not know what to say, but offered, "I am very, very sorry to learn this. So sorry for your loss."

She said, "I am glad you called. I have had no one to talk with."

After another pause she continued, "Frau Mueller has a Schwester who lives in Wells County. If I could contact her maybe she would be able to help Frau Mueller und die Kinder. But I do not know her ad-dress or if she has a telephone. I would like to talk with her or send a letter. I have asked Frau Mueller but all she says is her sister's name and the county where she lives."

He asked, "What is her sister's name? I will ask May to look into this and maybe locate a woman with that name in Wells County."

Gerde replied with some hope in her voice for the first time during the conversation. "Would you be willing to do that? Ich ware Ihnen sehr grateful. Sie ist geboren Mathilda Lehmann, but now Sie heist Mathilda Bauer and lives in Wells County. I heard Herr Mueller say that more than once when he was alive."

He wrote this information on a piece of paper and tucked the paper into his pocket. "I will work with May tomorrow to try to locate your Aunt's sister. One of us will call you to let you know what we learn."

She replied, "Danke, danke, danke."

He concluded by saying, "I am so very sorry for your loss. I wish I could have met your mother to tell her how special her daughter is. But I am sure she knew that."

"Vielen Dank," she said with a pained voice.

He heard the telephone disconnect.

The conversation with Gerde left him saddened and exhausted. He decided to delay calling his own brother for another day. He had no desire to do any more at his office that evening. He walked to his room and prepared for bed. Before turning out the light, however, he again read the page in his medical journal with the notice about a public health training program at Yale.

CHAPTER SIXTEEN

December 23, 1918

After Thanksgiving, the days leading up to Christmas seemed less festive in 1918 than in preceding years. Although the number of influenza cases had declined, deaths from the disease were still occurring. The schools were opened again the first week of December. Saturday classes had been added to make up some of the instruction time lost during the seven weeks of closure. Even though the quarantine ordinance was relaxed by mid-December, partly at the behest of shop owners who had been seeing few people in their stores, the number of shoppers during the week before Christmas continued to be much smaller than had been anticipated. Many townspeople seemed to have become accustomed to avoiding places where more than two or three people might gather.

Still, many residents of Rosebud County kept plans to celebrate Christmas, Hanukkah, and New Year's. The war had ended. No draftees had gone to military assignments since Armistice Day.

Doctor Harvey stood beside Frances Olson outside Howard School to welcome students back to classes and greet those parents who had brought their children to school. She said, "Some parents won't allow their children to return to school yet, but as you can see many have. Not all believe the danger is over."

He responded, "The epidemic does seem to be waning and it is reasonable to allow children to be in school again. But the danger is not over. We still rely on parents to keep ill children home. If a student is ill at school, teachers must isolate them and make arrangements for them to go home. I hope it does not become necessary to close schools again."

Frances replied, "I certainly hope not! Many business owners and parents were relieved when the ordinance was rescinded. I even heard Sheriff Starr say he was glad to have all his staff back again instead of 'quarantining', as he called it."

"I expect the county commissioners and city aldermen will be happy to concentrate on other issues, too," he said. "Not all business owners feel relieved though. Saloon operators won't have much of a chance to resume their normal practices before the state prohibition law closes them down for good at the end of the year. Like jumping from the frying pan into the fire, I guess. For them the dry new year may not be a happy one."

She responded wryly, "Even when the saloons are closed I expect liquor sales will not dry up entirely."

He asked, "Is enrollment at the smaller schools in the county expected to be about the same as it was before October?"

"I think it will be close to the same," she replied. "Some homesteader and rancher families have found places to live closer to town so their older children will be nearer to schools."

He observed, "It is no small sacrifice for families to arrange for their children to attend school."

"Must be doubly challenging in the middle of winter," she noted. "Thank you for being here. I'll let you know the enrollment numbers after I receive attendance reports from all the schools later this week."

On the morning of December 23, Doctor Harvey met the county commissioner on the sidewalk. "Good morning, Doctor. I am on my way to the café. Would you join me for a cup of coffee?"

"I would love to have some coffee to get the day started right."

"That's great. Let's go get some!"

They sat at a table by the window at the café. Alice greeted them. "Gentlemen, good to see you this morning. Would you like some coffee?"

Both said, "Yes, please."

She filled two cups and placed a creamer and sugar bowl on the table. The two men sipped their coffee and sat back in their chairs.

The commissioner spoke first. "Is this damned epidemic over? It has been a royal pain in the ass, a doozy of difficulty, for our county and the whole country."

Doctor Harvey responded, "For the whole world! This has been a pandemic, as big as epidemics get. It's not over but at least around here it has slowed down. It might resurge, but if we are lucky it will end soon."

"Lucky?" the commissioner said. "Isn't there something besides luck we can use to fight this?"

He replied, "Well, commissioner, the measures in the ordinance you passed probably helped slow the spread of disease and saved some lives. But until the exact cause of influenza is determined and maybe a vaccine developed, luck will remain an important ally."

The commissioner asked, "Do I understand correctly the hospital activity at the Masonic Lodge may be decommissioned soon?"

He replied, "I think so, although I have mixed feelings about losing the availability of a hospital setting here. The Masonic Lodge space has been very helpful, and having nurses to provide inpatient care has certainly saved some lives. It would be best if Forsyth had a hospital. Still, the temporary setting at the Masonic Lodge will probably end soon if influenza case counts continue to decline."

The commissioner said, "Commissioners have discussed this. Voters may agree to bonding to build a hospital, but I don't think the political will is firm enough yet to put this issue on a ballot."

Doctor Harvey added, "Some wounded and disabled young men will be returning from military facilities. The problems they bring will require substantial care and support. For some of these men availability of a hospital and nursing care may become the factor allowing them to stay in their hometowns or forcing them to relocate to cities with more capacity to support their needs."

"Good point, Doctor," the commissioner said. "We supported our young men on the way to war and need to support them when they return."

"There is one other item I'd like you to consider," he mentioned. "The nurses who have provided care at the emergency hospitals have all done an outstanding job. I think each would feel honored to receive a letter of commendation and thanks from the county commissioners.

I would be happy to draft a letter if the commissioners would consider issuing such a commendation."

The commissioner smiled, a rare display for him, and said, "Indeed. Please do. I am sure we will want to provide this recognition. While we are at it we'll want to document our thanks to the Masons, too."

Doctor Harvey replied, "Of course."

The commissioner finished his coffee and placed a dollar on the table before standing to leave. He said, "Thank you for the updates. I must go now."

Doctor Harvey waited at the table for a moment, then saw Alice coming. He said, "I have missed seeing you for a few months. I hope to come in regularly again now. Is the meatloaf still on the menu?"

"We have missed seeing you, too, Doctor. This disease has changed many things in our town. Do you think we'll ever get back to normal again?" she asked.

He opted not to pursue a discussion of normal.

She continued, "Yes, the meatloaf dish will be ready for you whenever you come. That's a part of normal we have not changed."

He asked, "Is the hamburger sandwich on the lunch menu?"

She responded, "Yes. We are calling hamburgers hamburgers again. Haven't heard anything about the Loyalty League lately, and don't really expect to hear more. Hope to see you at lunch, too."

He said, "Thanks. I'm looking forward to that."

He put on his coat and gloves and left the café.

When he arrived at his office May was sitting at her desk in the entry. She said, "Good morning. Did you freeze outside this morning?"

"Almost to the bone," he replied. "However, I just had coffee with the commissioner and I've begun to thaw. How are you today?"

"I feel fine," she said. "I am blessed to be healthy and working. I've been thinking about my wish for the New Year. Usually I wish for new and exciting experiences, but this year I'm hoping for 1919 to be less eventful and much less stressful than 1918!"

He responded, "I hope you get your wish! Many others will have the same hope."

May said, "The first scheduled visit today is at 1:30, so you have some time to review a few messages from this morning. There is nothing urgent."

"Good," he said. "I have wanted to talk with you about how you tracked down Jana Mueller's sister. You have certainly helped the Mueller family adapt, for now at least, to otherwise grim circumstances."

May began to recall her search for the sister and said, "Well, after Thanksgiving, when you told me of the difficulties Gerde was having, I began looking for a way to help. All we knew about the sister then was her married name and the county where she lived. I knew there was no Wells County in Montana. I called a friend who works at the state library in Helena. She and I took some classes together at MSC before I married and came to Forsyth. Only one year of college for me, but my friend graduated and became a librarian. It was fun to talk with her again.

"Anyway I asked her if she could find a Wells County in another state. She searched and called me back. She found two Wells Counties, one in North Dakota and one in Indiana. She also asked if I might be looking for Weld County in Colorado. I told her I'd start with the Wells Counties and probably begin in North Dakota. She told me the county seat there is Fessenden and even found a telephone number for the county auditor's office.

"When I called, a very friendly lady answered. I introduced myself and explained I was searching for a Mathilda Bauer, whose sister lives in our county in Montana. I told her I thought a woman with a German married name might not be too hard to locate. She laughed and said, 'You came to the right county to find German names. Almost everyone here is German, although there are a few Norwegians like me, too.'

"Then she asked how old Mathilda Bauer was. I told her probably about thirty to thirty-five years of age. She said, 'There are many Mathildas and more than one Mathilda Bauer in our county. I think you might be looking for Mathilda Bauer who lives up by Hamberg. She's about thirty-five, maybe forty years of age. The other Mathilda Bauers I know of are older women or young girls.'

"Then I asked if she knew whether or not this Mathilda had a telephone. She said, 'I don't think so but I could do a little checking and get back to you.'

"I thanked her for what she was doing. I also mentioned that if she found Mathilda Bauer has a sister Jana Mueller, born Jana Lehmann, then she might want to tell Mathilda her sister Jana is alive—although she did lose her husband in October."

Doctor Harvey was fascinated by May's tale of sleuthing. He said, "You may have missed your calling. Many a Pinkerton would be envious of your detective work. Did the Wells County Auditor's Office get back to you?"

May, who was obviously enjoying the opportunity to share her adventure, responded, "Oh, yes. She called. I had called her on a Tuesday and she called back on that Friday. Mathilda Bauer does not have a telephone but the lady from the auditor's office had driven to her home. I do believe the folks in North Dakota may be the most helpful people on earth. And sure enough, Mathilda Bauer near Hamberg, North Dakota, is the older sister of Jana Mueller, who came with her husband to Rosebud County, Montana."

Doctor Harvey said, "I am aware Gerde, Mrs. Mueller, and the children went to the sister's home in North Dakota before Christmas. Were you involved with making that arrangement?"

May replied, "Yes. I helped and so did the lady at the Wells County Auditor's Office. She arranged for Mathilda Bauer to be at the auditor's office at a time Gerde called. I was told the entire conversation was in German and involved quite a mixture of tears and joy. Mrs. Mueller's sister invited the Mueller family to come for Christmas. Fessenden is on the Milwaukee Road line, so the Mueller family took the train right from here to there."

He marveled at how much May had done to help. He said, "Apparently Gerde has returned to Rosebud County to try to keep the Mueller ranch operating. She is a very brave young woman, but I'm not so sure she can succeed at this."

May responded, "I would not count her out. She has developed an arrangement with a hired hand, a young man from a German homesteader family up by Ingomar. I guess his family has decided to return to Iowa but he wants to stay. Whether or not Jana Mueller returns, Gerde wants to keep the ranch in the family. And she is trying to find a way to have her own sister and brother come from Germany to Rosebud County."

"Are you helping her with that, too?"

May replied, "Yes. The more involved I become with the Mueller family, the more I want to do. It makes me feel good to help them."

He said with admiration, "It's lucky for them you are here. Your dedication balances some of the unfair treatment they've experienced, although nothing can fully compensate their loss to the influenza epidemic. Let me also say that while the folks in North Dakota have been very, very helpful, when it comes to looking for the most helpful person on earth, the search party won't need to look any further than where you are sitting!"

He continued, "Thank you for your work. I will review those messages now."

However, he hesitated before going into the examination room. All morning he had had a headache. It had become more painful, and now he was sure he also had a fever.

He said to May, "I may be coming down with something myself. I have a fever and a headache. Would you try to contact the patients scheduled this afternoon and tomorrow morning and reschedule their visits until after Christmas? It might be best if I isolate myself the rest of today to see if I develop a cough. I wouldn't want to spread anything to my patients."

May appeared concerned by the idea he might be ill. She knew he had worked very long hours every day since the epidemic had come in October. But the physician was not supposed to be vulnerable.

She said, "Surely, I will reschedule the appointments. Is there anything else I can do to help?"

"I'll just go to my room and get some rest this afternoon," he replied. "I'm sure I will be feeling better tomorrow morning."

She looked out the window. "It has started to snow. You should get your coat on and go now. I'll contact the patients and close the office this afternoon."

He went into the examination room, picked up the messages from his desk, and donned his warm winter coat.

When he walked by May's desk she asked, "Do you remember when we talked after Armistice Day? You said something about a red horse supporting a pale horse. What did you mean?"

He looked at his ever curious and always helpful assistant. He replied, "I do remember. We have seen the red horse and also a white horse; the sword and pestilence are affecting more than a fourth of the earth. The pale horse has been busy."

He took a piece of paper from her desk, wrote something on it, and handed it to her. Then he said, "When you are home tonight read this."

May looked at him and at the paper. She said, "These are Bible verses."

"Yes," he said as he stepped out the door.

In his room at the Alexander Hotel Annex he looked at the bottle of Flying U whiskey, but a drink did not appeal to him. He wanted to think as clearly as possible. He thought his headache and fever would probably resolve once he had a good night of sleep. As long as he did not develop a cough or upper respiratory congestion, he would return to his office to see patients right after Christmas.

He thought of preparing a letter to request information about admission to the public health program at Yale University. He had listed some of the questions he would ask. The letter would go to C-E. A. Winslow at the Department of Public Health, Yale School of Medicine, New Haven, Connecticut. But he needed to get some rest now. He would prepare the letter tomorrow.

Before he went to bed he read the verses in his Bible he had cited to May: Revelation 6: 2, 4, 8.

He also looked at the cover of a novel sent to him by a friend from medical school. His friend had recently returned to Chicago from France, where he had served in the Army Medical Corps at a military hospital caring for wounded and ill soldiers. The novel by a Spanish author, Ibáñez, had been translated to English, *The Four Horsemen of the Apocalypse*. His friend had included a handwritten note in the book.

"See what Tchernoff says at the end of Part 1. While I was in Europe I saw all this: pestilence, war, famine, and death."

Doctor Harvey thought, *I have seen much of this, too. While the black horse of famine has not come to Rosebud County, an epidemic of suspicion has been added to the pestilence and war of our time. Could pestilence and epidemics such as these be prevented, or at least better controlled?*

He went to bed and soon fell asleep.

He awoke to the familiar *knock, knock, knock* and the voice of the hotel owner's son. "Doctor Harvey, are you there?" Then silence.

Doctor Harvey could not move or speak. He could not open his eyes.

Later he heard *knock, knock, knock,* again, and then the door opening. The voice this time was the hotel owner's. "Doctor Harvey, are you all right?"

CHAPTER SEVENTEEN

January 1919

He sat motionless, his eyes closed. What was that smell? An antiseptic? He heard a voice he recognized. It was May. Who was she talking to?

"He was found in his room at the hotel on Christmas Eve," said May. "One physician in Forsyth thought he had had a stroke, but the signs were very unusual. We brought him here by train on Christmas Day."

Another woman replied, "His case has been a mystery here, too. We can get him to open his eyes by nudging him persistently. Then we can feed him by mouth. We take him to the bathroom and keep nudging him while he sits to urinate or defecate. But we must keep nudging or he closes his eyes and is motionless again except for the tremor of his fingers."

May said, "We couldn't provide the nursing care you are giving. I am so glad we brought him to Deaconess Hospital in Billings."

Doctor Harvey thought, *Deaconess Hospital? Billings?*

He felt someone pushing on his shoulder. They pushed harder and shook his shoulder. He opened his eyes. The room was bright. He saw May, a woman in a nurse's uniform, and a man in a gray dress suit. He wanted to greet May but he couldn't speak. He closed his eyes again.

A man spoke, "I have talked with colleagues in Denver and Minneapolis as well as my colleagues here in Billings. We have all scratched our heads about this case. But I believe we have a diagnosis now."

Diagnosis? thought Doctor Harvey. *What has happened to me?*

The man continued, "I found an article in the *American Journal of*

Medical Sciences by Skversky about an illness occurring in the American Expeditionary Force in Europe and then found case reports about what seems to be the same illness in this country in New York, Pennsylvania, Maine, Indiana, Michigan, and Texas. We may be working with that syndrome here. The cases have fever followed by pathologic drowsiness, difficulty walking, and marked Parkinsonian signs.

"The syndrome has a name, given by an Austrian neurologist who has seen cases in Europe. It is 'encephalitis lethargica.' Looks like there is a widespread epidemic of this. Might be related to the Spanish flu, but probably not. Just what we needed—another epidemic."

May said softly, "The white horse is not finished yet."

The man continued, "We'll keep providing careful nursing, a nutritious diet, hydrotherapy, and massage. Recovery can occur from a few days to a month, but some cases have had protracted illness from many weeks to several months."

Doctor Harvey thought, *Syndrome? Another epidemic? Recovery takes weeks? I must recover and finish the letter to Yale.*

December 1969

Doctor Harvey watched as two women approached him. He then gazed down at the wheelchair in which he was sitting and at his own hands and arms. The shining metal frame of the chair appeared new, but his hands and arms were old, thin, and wrinkled. He moved his hands from the arms of the chair onto his bone-thin legs. He looked around the room, which was lined by two rows of single beds, six in each row. Electric lights suspended from the high ceiling illuminated the room, as did daylight through several mullioned windows on one side. Other men dressed like him were sitting on beds or walking around the room. One of the women approaching him wore a nurse's uniform. He realized he was a patient in a hospital.

The other woman was wearing a blue dress, with the hem extending to mid-calf and the sleeves to mid-forearm. It was buttoned in front from the collar area to mid-bust and appeared warm, although the fabric was not wool. She wore a thin silver necklace and glasses with thin silver-colored rims. Her gray hair was combed back and extended below her ears but not to her shoulders. Her solid black shoes were each secured with a three-row shoelace and supported in back by a two-inch heel. She had a confident posture and steady gait. Her facial features, especially her eyes, were familiar. Did he know her?

She asked, "Doctor Harvey? Ist Sie das? Is it you?"

When he heard her voice he knew who she was. "Gerde," he said. "It is so good to see you. You are older, yet your eyes, your voice. It is you!"

He extended his hands and she grasped them. Tears streamed down her face and down his.

"Gerde. How are you?"

"I am fine. I thought I would never see you again."

She leaned forward and hugged him.

"Where are we and how did you find me?" he asked.

"We are at the State Hospital in Warm Springs," she replied. "I received a letter from a doctor here. I could hardly believe what I read. Now I see it is true."

She leaned forward again and hugged him even more tightly.

"The letter said you had not spoken and rarely moved since you came here and were given a new medication. Once you spoke you said my name, Gerde, Gerde Mueller. You said you wanted someone to let me know you were here."

The woman in the nurse's uniform said, "Yes, Doctor Harvey, Gerde still lives in Forsyth and we were able to find her. We have wanted to talk with you for a long time. Now it looks like we finally can. There is much the doctors and nurses would like to learn. You have an unusual condition, encephalitis lethargica, and because of this you have been unable to talk or move. One of our doctors learned of a breakthrough in treating this condition. At a hospital in New York City a new medication was given to patients with your condition, and they responded in a remarkable way. And you have also responded. Some of us feel this has been almost a miracle. We are all thrilled to get to know you."

He was trying to comprehend what he was being told. Neither smiling nor frowning, he stared intensely at the nurse. When he shifted his gaze to Gerde he felt relief and a need to learn what had happened to her, to May, and to others from Forsyth while he had been away.

A flood of questions began to flow. "Gerde, did your sister and brother come to live with you? How is Jana Mueller? How is May? Have the sedition accusations ceased? Is sauerkraut, not liberty cabbage, on the menu at the café? Is there a hospital in Forsyth? Oh, I have so many questions. How long will you be able to visit?"

Gerde looked fondly at him. "Ja, meine Schwester und mein Bruder came to Montana."

She paused before continuing, "But I am sorry to say Frau Mueller and May have both died. The sedition talk ended, but it ruined so many lives. Some of those convicted spent years in prison at Deer Lodge only a few miles from here."

Tears welled up in her eyes. "There was another war, again with Germany but also with Japan. Japanese Americans were moved from their homes and confined to camps in Wyoming, Idaho, and other states."

"Oh my," he said. "Another war? Liberties deprived again?"

"Ja, and yet another war is happening now. There is so much to tell."

Gerde then asked the nurse, "Is there a more private place where we could talk?"

"Of course, come with me," she replied as she began to push the wheelchair with Doctor Harvey toward the door to leave the large room.

He asked, "May I have a writing tablet and a pencil? I want to write down what I am remembering."

"Of course," the nurse replied again.

As they approached the door he was thinking, *I remember listening to nurses at Deaconess Hospital. I remember the railway station and many Forsyth people who were there. I remember Marie.* He felt very sad but continued his thoughts, *Oh my, I am so old now.*

Gerde said softly, "Das Leben ist ungerecht. So much of life has not been fair."

He thought about this, *Fair? I guess not. I had a longer life than did Marie or our unborn baby. I bore different burdens than did Mr. Mueller or Gerde. Not every painter is a Michelangelo or every writer a Shakespeare. Maybe the white-robed Fates spun and wove the thread of life? If so I must record my memories before the inevitable cut of that thread.*

Afterword

The Montana Sedition Law, passed in February 1918, was not repealed until 1973, when the state's criminal codes were revised. However, after the armistice of November 1918, the Montana Council of Defense and the Montana Loyalty League continued to focus attention on radical labor groups, such as the Industrial Workers of the World, while anti-German activity declined. Still, seventy-nine people were convicted of sedition and forty-seven were imprisoned, with sentences up to twenty years as a result of the civil liberty–crushing xenophobia. Not until 2006 were seventy-eight of those convicted pardoned posthumously by Governor Brian Schweitzer, who is the grandson of German-Russian immigrants.

Cases of Spanish influenza continued to occur in Montana through the summer of 1919, although the number of cases decreased dramatically after the epidemic peaked in October and November 1918. The cause of influenza in humans, a virus, was not identified until 1933. An effective vaccine to protect against influenza was not developed until 1938 and not licensed by the FDA until 1945.

A hospital was opened in Forsyth in 1921 after campaigns using the slogan "Remember the 1918 Flu Epidemic" garnered the support needed to pass the necessary bonding authority in 1919 and 1920.

The syndrome encephalitis lethargica affected thousands of people around the world from 1915 until the mid-1920s. Some of those with this syndrome recovered within weeks or a few months; others developed a severe condition in which their bodies were frozen with rigidity. This severe catatonic syndrome required institutional care for many. In the late 1960s some survivors were revived by use of the drug L-dopa. Neurologist Oliver Sacks, in his book *Awakenings* (1973), described the near-miraculous response to this drug of some of these patients. The cause of the syndrome remains unknown.

If Doctor Harvey had recovered from encephalitis lethargica and enrolled in a public health training program such as the one launched at Yale University in 1915, he would have had the opportunity to participate in delivering extraordinary public health achievements in the twentieth century. These achievements include decreased maternal, fetal, and infant mortality and increased life expectancy in the United States. Recognition and treatment of diseases such as diabetes mellitus, tuberculosis, and many others improved dramatically. Preventive steps, particularly the use of vaccines, saved millions of lives.

The behaviors stimulated by fear, anxiety, and beliefs related to war and disease described in this story were not unique to the early twentieth century.

Acknowledgments

This historical novella depicts fictional characters responding to events that occurred in eastern Montana in 1917 and 1918. I have attempted to construct dialogue and a story consistent with the experience of people living in rural Montana during the years of World War I and the Spanish flu epidemic.

My version of these events was greatly aided by very helpful staff at the Rosebud County Courthouse, the Rosebud County Pioneer Museum, and the Rosebud County Library and by equally helpful staff at the Montana Historical Society and the Gallatin County History Museum. The editors and production staff at Sweetgrass Books provided invaluable assistance.

This work is dedicated to my wife, Linda E. Quist Ortmeyer, whose maternal grandparents homesteaded in Rosebud County during the 1910s and 1920s. Her tolerance for my frequent preoccupation with this story made the book possible.

Sources

Forsyth, Rosebud County, Rural Montana

Coates, D. "A Guide to Historic Forsyth, City of Trees." 8-page brochure. forsythmt.com/documents/forsyth%20walking%20tour.pdf.

Forsyth City Directory, 1916. R. L. Polk and Co. 1916.

Forsyth Democrat, weekly issues, 1917-1918. Rosebud County Library.

Forsyth Times-Journal, weekly issues 1917-1918. Rosebud County Library.

Grana, M. *Pioneer Doctor. The Story of a Woman's Work.* TwoDot Publishing, Helena, MT. 2005.

Gray, D. *Nothing to Tell: Extraordinary Stories of Montana Ranch Women.* TwoDot Publishing, Helena, MT. 2012.

Hill, J. J. "Going public. Childbirth, the Board of Health, and Montana women, 1860-1920." *Montana The Magazine of Western History.* 2015. 65: 3-21.

Luther, N. Forsyth and Rosebud newspaper index 1894-1924. Buggles Publishing, Forsyth, MT. 2003.

Mercier, L. "Surviving Montana. Women's memories of work and family life, 1900-1960." *Montana The Magazine of Western History.* 2015. 65: 25-46.

Minnick, R. P. *A Doctor on the Last Frontier: Memoirs of a Montana Physician*. Pioneer Publishing Co., Fresno, CA. 1989.

Raymer, R. G. *Montana The Land and the People*. Montana biography (3 volumes). The Lewis Publishing Co., Chicago. 1930.

Rosebud County Bicentennial Committee. *They Came and Stayed. Rosebud County History*. Western Publishing and Lithography, Billings, MT. 1977.

Sanders, H. F. *A History of Montana* (3 volumes). The Lewis Publishing Co., Chicago. 1913.

Schwantes, C. A., Ronda, J. P. *The West the Railroads Made*. University of Washington Press, Seattle. 2008.

Spanagel, D. T., Guptil, J. S. *Trials and Triumphs. A 200 Year History of the Exploration and Development of an Area Along the Yellowstone River, Touching the Lives of the Settlers and their Descendents*. S&G Printshop, Jordan, MT. 1994.

Influenza Pandemic

Barry, J. M. *The Great Influenza. The Epic Story of the Deadliest Plague in History*. Viking, New York. 2004.

Dicke, T. "Waiting for the Flu. Inertia and the Spanish Influenza Pandemic, 1918-1919." *Journal of the History of Medicine and Allied Sciences*. 2015. 70: 195-217.

Montana State Board of Health. Minutes of October 9, 1918 meeting. Montana Historical Society library.

Mullen, P. C., Nelson, M. L. "Montanans and 'the most peculiar disease.' The influenza epidemic and public health, 1918-1919. *Montana The Magazine of Western History*. 1987. Spring: 50-61.

Porter, K. A. *Pale Horse, Pale Rider in the Collected Stories of Katherine Anne Porter*. A Harvest Book, Harcourt, Inc., New York. 1944.

Schafer, J. A. "Fighting for business: The limits of professional coopera-tion among American doctors during the First World War." *Journal of the History of Medicine and Allied Sciences.* 2015. 70: 165-194.

Thompson, G. D. C. *50 Year History of the Montana State Board of Health, 1901-1951.* Montana Historical Society library.

Encephalitis Lethargica

Economo, C. v. "Die encephalitis lethargica. Jahrbucher fur Phsychiatrie," Leipzig und Wien. 1917-1918. xxxviii: 253.

Sacks, O. *Awakenings.* Duckworth & Company, London. 1973.

Skversky, A. "Lethargic encephalitis in the A. E. F.: A clinical study." *The American Journal of Medical Sciences.* 1919. clviii: 849.

Sedition Concerns

Malone, M. P., Roeder, R. B., Lang, W. L. *Montana: A History of Two Centuries* (revised edition). University of Washington Press. Seattle. 1991.

Work, C. P. *Darkest Before Dawn. Sedition and Free Speech in the American West.* University of New Mexico Press, Albuquerque. 2005.

Other

Articles in the *Journal of the American Medical Association* such as: "Therapeutics, disturbances of the kidneys." *JAMA.* 1917. LXVIII: 1257-1258 or "The medical officer of the Army, sanitary service in the field." JAMA. 1917. LXVIII: 1259-1261.

Dirschl, D. R. "Surgical irrigation of open fractures—a change in prac-tice?" *New England Journal of Medicine.* 2015. 373: 2680-2681.

Eknoyan, G. "A history of edema and its management." Kidney International. 1997. 59: S118-126.

Gillet, M. C. *The Army Medical Department, 1917-1941.* Center for Military History, Washington, DC. 2009.

Grimes, J., ed. *Sexually Transmitted Disease. An Encyclopedia of Diseases, Prevention, Treatment, and Issues.* Greenwood Press, Santa Barbara, CA. 2014.

Hull, A. J. "The cure of inguinal hernia." *British Medical Journal.* 1917. 2: 548-550.

Ibanez, V. B. *The Four Horsemen of the Apocalypse* (translated by Charlotte Brewster Jordan). A. L. Burt Company, New York. 1918.

Lee, F. S. *Scientific Features of Modern Medicine.* Columbia University Press, New York. 1911.

Mazur, A. "Why were 'starvation diets' promoted for diabetes in the pre-insulin period?" *Nutrition Journal.* 2011. 10: 23-55.

About the Author

Steven Helgerson was born in Washington. He received degrees from the University of Puget Sound and the University of Washington. His medical specialty is preventive medicine. During a forty-year career in public health he worked with the Centers for Disease Control and Prevention, the Centers for Medicare and Medicaid Services, and the Indian Health Service as well as several state and local health departments. From 2006 to 2015 he served as the Montana State Medical Officer. He lives in Seattle.